STORM OVER GOLD ROCK

Deputy Marshal Mick Nelson is escorting captured outlaws when the train they are travelling in is derailed. The outlaws escape, taking a young girl as hostage, and Mick sets off in pursuit. He follows the outlaws across country, meeting a strange sect who have acquired the girl from the outlaws. Mick tracks the outlaws to Gold Rock, a remote and hostile gold rush town. Besieged on all sides, he faces an almost impossible task with only determination and his gun-skill to help him. Can he win through ... and survive?

STORM OVER GOLD ROCK

by

L. D. Tetlow

Dales Large Print Books
Long Preston, North Yorkshire,
BD23 4ND, England.

British Library Cataloguing in Publication Data.

Tetlow, L. D.
    Storm over Gold Rock.

    A catalogue record of this book is
    available from the British Library

    ISBN   1-84262-077-0 pbk

First published in Great Britain 2000
by Robert Hale Limited

Published in Large Print 2001 by arrangement with
Robert Hale Limited

Dales Large Print is an imprint of Library Magna Books Ltd.

Printed and bound in Great Britain by
T.J. (International) Ltd., Cornwall, PL28 8RW

ONE

It had been a long and boring train journey for Deputy Marshal Mick Nelson and he was not in the best of tempers. The train had arrived in the town of Greenhills almost three hours behind schedule, although the local sheriff, one Dan Spencer, did assure Mick that this was quite normal. He even claimed that the train was in fact early, since it usually arrived about five hours late. This piece of information did little to placate Mick Nelson.

Mick had been sent to Greenhills to collect two outlaws, Saul Evans and Harold Buck, both wanted in connection with several murders and armed robbery. Escorting prisoners was a job Mick hated but, as a relatively junior deputy marshal, he had little say in where he was sent and for what.

After checking on his charges in the local jail and confirming that they were who Sheriff Dan Spencer claimed they were, Mick had time on his hands. He passed most of that evening in the only saloon in Greenhills, owned by a man whose appearance convinced Mick that should he delve far enough back amongst Wanted posters, he would discover that he too was wanted somewhere for something.

He was due to leave Greenhills the following afternoon on the noon southbound train. It might have been due to leave Greenhills at noon but if the northbound journey was anything to go by and what was obviously the accepted late running of the train, it would be closer to six in the evening before the train even arrived.

He took a quick walk around the town, which did not take very long since it consisted of only one main street, two short side streets with several dark alleys leading off to various houses, and the railroad station. Most of the houses appeared to be little more than back-to-back shacks, although some did have a small back yard. He very quickly came to the decision that Greenhills was one of the bleakest, saddest-looking towns that he had ever visited. Even the residents seemed bleak and sad and he did not see anyone smile the whole time he was there. He put this down to the conditions in which most of them lived.

The only friendly face he met belonged to a mongrel dog which wagged its tail furiously and greeted him with a yap and what could only be described as a laughing face. He patted the dog, which seemed to be a mistake since it obviously took this as sign of encouragement and attached itself to him for the remainder of that evening. It apparently waited outside the saloon for him to reappear.

It was not difficult to see what most folk in Greenhills did for a living as there was a large lumber mill on the edge of town and, according to Sheriff Spencer, some work was available on a few farms further away from the town. It was obvious that many people were employed as lumberjacks in the surrounding forest and others in the lumber yard itself. Indeed, timber appeared to be the main export from the town since there were several railroad flat wagons laden with sawn timbers in a marshalling yard at the side of the mill. The area was completely surrounded by forest stretching as far as the eye could see and it had seemed to Mick that he had been travelling through forest for the greater part of his journey.

Before walking round the town and then going into the saloon, Mick was, grudgingly it seemed, given a meal cooked by the sheriff's wife. Since the town did not support a hotel and the only other accommodation available was a run-down rooming-house, his overnight accommodation consisted of a rough bed in the sheriff's office, and this was where his meal was served.

There was certainly no suggestion that he might like to spend the evening in the comfort of the sheriff's house, which was one of the better properties in Greenhills. It seemed that as far as Sheriff Dan Spencer was concerned, doing his duty in arresting the outlaws and notifying the necessary authorities, was all he needed to do and he had no intention of co-operating further.

Mick certainly did not enjoy what purported to be beef and dumpling stew but could have been almost anything as far as he was concerned. The beef was tough and gristly and the dumplings might have been better employed as cannonballs. Unfortunately he had little choice and was forced to accept what was offered since there was no dining establishment in town and by that time all the stores had closed. Mrs Spencer was certainly not the best cook he had ever met although he had to admit that he had been offered worse on occasion. Even though he was hungry he was unable to finish it all, especially most of the very tough meat, although he did manage to force some of the dumplings into his complaining stomach. Even the coffee tasted odd, which was one of the reasons he decided to go into the saloon.

Like the rest of the town, the saloon was shabby, very dingy and rather dirty with a resident population of cockroaches vying for spilt beer. The home-brewed beer came up to what he considered the standard of the town – cloudy and tasting like washing up slops but the cockroaches did not appear to mind. After one glass of slops he transferred to whiskey. Even that did not appear to be such a good idea at first; the whiskey was local moonshine, very rough and strong, but after a few sips his palate became deadened and it even began to taste quite good. It was certainly better than the beer and Mrs Spencer's coffee.

To pass the time he played a few games of cards with a couple of locals. Although they were only playing for pennies the two locals seemed to take it very seriously. Mick had the feeling that he was playing against the two men combined since he lost almost every hand. However, he chose not to challenge what he considered cheating on the part of his two companions. It hardly seemed worth the bother.

His faithful new companion greeted him warmly when he eventually emerged from the saloon and Mick wondered if the animal belonged to anyone and if it had been fed. He had been given a key to the sheriff's office and let himself in and was pleased and surprised to discover that the stove had been lit. He took pity on the dog which stood hopefully at the door looking pleadingly at him and he allowed it into the office. It was plainly used to not being allowed inside any building.

He had expected the remains of his meal to have been cleared away but it was still there, festering on the desk. He looked at the plate, at the dog, smiled, and placed the plate on the floor. It seemed that the dog appreciated Mrs Spencer's cooking even if he did not. After licking the plate clean the dog curled up in front of the stove and went to sleep. Mick once again took pity on the animal and allowed it to stay the night.

As he had crossed the street, Mick had been very conscious of the rising wind and the definite feeling that it was about to rain.

A sudden clap of thunder and the sound of heavy rain confirmed his feeling.

'What the hell is that thing doin' in here?' demanded Sheriff Spencer when he entered the office shortly after dawn. The dog needed no telling to leave and, cowering low, made its escape, expertly darting between the sheriff's legs, something it appeared to have done on more than one occasion.

'I invited it in,' said Mick. 'He was the only decent company I had all night. Who owns him?'

'Nobody,' said the sheriff. 'Blasted nuisance he can be. I've tried to shoot him a couple of times but I'll swear he knows what's in my mind before I do sometimes. I did manage to get a line on him once but I reckon he can even dodge bullets. Good ratter though, I'll give him that.'

'Some dogs are like that,' said Mick. 'They seem to lead a charmed life. He strikes me as a good dog though. I would have thought somebody would have taken him in, especially if he's a good ratter.'

'You want him, you take him,' invited the sheriff. 'At least folk'll be able to leave their doors open without wonderin' if he'll get in

11

an' steal their food.'

'I'll think about it,' said Mick. 'I see it's rainin' an' the wind seems pretty strong and there's been thunder rollin' round all night. In fact I'd say it was blowin' up for a real wild one.'

'Seems like it,' grunted Spencer, apparently dismissing the fact as something quite normal. 'Mrs Spencer will be along with your breakfast in a while. I know she'll be glad when them two in there have gone. We don't get no money for feedin' them or you, you know.'

'That's the way things go,' said Mick. 'So what's the news on the train then? I don't suppose there's any chance that it might be runnin' to time?'

'It left Clovis an hour late last night accordin' to the telegraph clerk,' said the sheriff. 'I guess that means it'll reach here sometime about five tonight. It always loses time through the mountains. Sometimes it don't come at all, especially in the winter when the track gets covered in snow. Sometimes we don't get a train through for a week or two if the passes are blocked. Still, it ain't winter so you should be all right.' Mick sincerely hoped that it would arrive even if it was late. He had no desire to spend another two days in Greenhills, which was when the next southbound train was due.

Breakfast for him and the prisoners eventually arrived and, much to Mick's dismay, consisted of the same beef stew as the night before. He simply could not face it but his thoughts went to the dog and he decided that since he seemed to appreciate it he might as well have it when he had the opportunity to give it to him. The two prisoners also complained loudly but they did eat what they were given. Harold Buck even expressed his thanks, within earshot of the sheriff and Mrs Spencer, that he was being taken away and that wherever he was taken the food could not be any worse. Mrs Spencer was plainly not amused and stated that they were being given exactly the same as she and her husband ate. Expressions of sympathy for the sheriff did not serve to improve her mood.

The one thing Mick had seen in the town on his walkabout the previous evening was a bakery, although it had been closed at the time, as were the other stores. He lost no time in heading straight for it and buying two still-warm loaves one of which he would keep for later – and some butter and smoked ham from the general store next door. He then returned to the office to gorge himself.

His new-found friend had attached itself to his heels almost as soon as he had left the office and returned with him with an expectant look. Although the sheriff was not in the office, Mick did not want to risk the animal being shot should he suddenly appear and took the plate of stew round to the back of the office where he fed it to the grateful animal.

During the day the wind became much stronger and the rain heavier. At four o'clock Sheriff Spencer informed Mick that the train had just passed through Selma although he did not explain where Selma was and Mick did not bother to ask – and that it would arrive in Greenhills at about 5.30. Mick did not hold too much store by this fact, he would believe it when the train arrived and not before.

However, it was plain that the train would now arrive and he prepared his prisoners for their journey. Preparation involved attaching ankle and wrist shackles to each man with a strong chain between them. Evans and Buck objected and made assertions and threats that it would not be long before they were free. Mick had heard it all before and simply allowed them to rant on.

He was more than surprised when the sheriff's prediction as to when the train would arrive proved very accurate. It ground slowly into the tiny railroad station during a lull in the weather amid a lot of noise and blowing of whistles both from the train and a little, uniformed man who strutted the rough wooden deck of the platform very importantly. He made great show of giving a series of blasts on his whistle and waving a red flag – apparently an indication that the engineer must stop the train. Mick smiled at the display and wondered if the engineer really needed any flags or whistles to tell him when and where to stop.

The train consisted of four passenger carriages, one guard's van-cum-freight wagon and a flatbed which carried a strange shape covered in canvas. Since he was travelling at the state's expense, Mick had booked himself into the only first class carriage – which was the second carriage – for what would be at least a fifteen-hour journey. His prisoners would be shackled in the guard's van. The leading carriage, it appeared, was a private carriage.

Apart from the temporary lull when the train arrived, the wind and rain had been steadily increasing in intensity during the day and seemed to be threatening to demolish most of the shacks in Greenhills. Sheriff Spencer had also expressed concern at the change in the weather and for the first time admitted that he had not experienced winds or rain of this severity for at least ten years. At that time most of the town had apparently been destroyed and many folk made homeless. While Mick did not wish harm on anyone in Greenhills he privately thought that flattening the town might not be a bad thing.

His canine companion had hardly left his side all day and, as Mick loaded his charges in to the guard's van, the animal seemed to lose its smile and even looked very worried.

'Looks like this is where we part, feller,' said Mick, bending down to stroke the dog. 'You ought to find yourself a good owner.' The dog licked its lips, gave a little yap and shuffled its legs. 'Sorry feller,' continued Mick. 'Kind of life I lead don't leave much room for dogs. You just make sure you stay one jump ahead of that sheriff. He don't like dogs.'

At that moment the station master gave another ear-shattering blast on his whistle, yelled 'All aboard!' and waved his flag, this time a green one. Mick patted the dog again and leapt aboard the guard's van. The dog yapped and then whined loudly and, as the train began to move, started to run along-side. Mick watched it for a while thinking that it would soon give up the chase, but it seemed that he was wrong and he feared that it would run until it collapsed. Suddenly he was on his stomach and reaching out for the animal. It obviously realized what he was trying to do and hurled itself at his outstretched arms. For a moment it seemed that it would fall under the wheels but Mick managed to grab it by the scruff and hauled it aboard. It shook itself and looked at Mick with what seemed a trium-phant look on its face.

'OK, feller,' grunted Mick, 'you win. You'll have to stay here though, I don't think they like dogs where I'm sittin'. You can keep an eye on these two.' He indicated the prisoners. 'If they try to escape you just let me know.' He was, of course, joking, but the dog appeared to understand and sat itself down opposite the two outlaws and growled at them.

'Dogs is freight,' announced the guard as he slid the door across the wagon. 'Freight has to be paid for.'

'So bill the State Governor,' said Mick. 'He's the one pickin' up the tab, not me.' He thought for a moment. 'Maybe not though. OK, how much?'

The guard relaxed and smiled. 'I've seen that dog for about the last two years now,' he said. 'Nobody seems to know where he came from an' nobody seems to care. You're the first person I've ever seen who he really took a shine to. I reckon he was lookin' for an owner an' now he's found one. OK, the dog travels for nothin', just don't tell the president.'

'President?' queried Mick.

'Sure, we've got the president ridin' in the front car,' said the guard.

'The President of the United States!' exclaimed Mick, not believing his ears.

The guard laughed loudly. 'This president is far more important than the President of the United States, at least as far as I'm concerned,' he said. 'No, sir, not the President of the United States, the president of the railroad company.'

'I guess that explains a lot,' Mick smiled. 'I mean all that whistle blowin' and flag wavin' back at Greenhills. That was all show just to impress.'

'Yeh, I guess Jed Proctor did make a meal

of it,' said the guard.

'And what does your president think about the train bein' five an' a half hours behind schedule?'

'Don't know,' muttered the guard. 'It don't do for the likes of me to ask them kind of questions. Anyhow, it's nothin' to do with me, I don't drive the train.'

'Does he know he has two hardened outlaws on his train?' Mick asked. He had had a similar experience a few months previously and the gentleman concerned had even raised the matter with the state governor.

'Wouldn't know about that either,' replied the guard. 'I didn't even know myself until we arrived in Clovis. It don't bother me none though, I've transported prisoners before and I ain't never lost one yet.'

'There's a first time for everythin',' sneered Saul Evans.

'Like the hangman's rope,' said Mick. 'Only thing is, that'll also be your last time.' For no particular reason he checked on their shackles and chains and, satisfied that all was well, he bent down and stroked the dog. 'You just keep an eye on these two, don't let them escape.' The dog licked its lips and wagged its tail and settled down, its chin on the floor but its eyes staring unblinkingly at the outlaws.

'I guess there ain't no need for me to stay here,' he said to the guard. 'I'll be in the first class if you want me. I'll check on them in a couple of hours.'

'The next stop is Woodlake in about three hours,' said the guard. 'It's just a couple of small farms where we take on more fuel and water.'

'I'll probably come back and check on things then,' said Mick.

There were six other people in the first class: a lone, quite elderly looking woman, a younger couple, two well dressed men who were probably businessmen, and a very large, surly-looking man in the seat by the door which led through to the private carriage. Mick assumed that he was a bodyguard employed by the railroad company to look after their president. This assumption appeared confirmed when another man came from the private car and spoke to him. Mick sat himself on the opposite side of the carriage to the elderly woman.

'Pardon me, Marshal,' said the elderly woman after she had spent some time peering at Mick's badge of office. 'I couldn't help but see that you had two men in chains with you. Shouldn't you be keeping an eye on them. We don't want them breaking loose and murdering us all.'

'They won't get loose, ma'am,' assured Mick. 'Mind, if it'd make you feel any easier, I could bring them in here where I can keep watch on them.'

'There's no need to be facetious, young man,' she bridled. 'It has been known for such men to escape. I should know, my dear departed husband was a circuit judge.' Quite how this fact qualified her to know, Mick was uncertain, but he did not contradict her in any way. 'Are they dangerous men?' she asked.

'I'm takin' them back to answer charges of at least four murders an' several charges of robbery,' replied Mick. 'I wouldn't let it worry you though, ma'am, they're well chained up.' He changed the subject. 'I hear we've got the president of the railroad company up front. I'll bet he has somethin' to say about the times this train keeps to. It's more than five hours late already.'

'I know,' she sniffed. 'It's disgraceful. In fact I have already mentioned it to him when he came through some time ago. He didn't seem particularly interested. Four

21

murders,' she said. 'Let's just hope that they don't get the opportunity to do any more. I still think you should be back there with them. It comes to something when the authorities pay first class for someone to escort prisoners, a deputy marshal at that.'

'We all have to start somewhere,' said Mick. 'I'll be a fully fledged marshal one day. I don't suppose that your husband started out as a judge.'

'That's different,' she sniffed.

All conversation in the carriage ceased and, despite the jolting caused mainly by the high winds, Mick later discovered that he had gone to sleep. He was only really made aware of this fact when the train ground to a halt. A glance at his pocket watch told him that it was a little over three hours since they had left Greenhills and a battered sign, just visible in the light from the carriage, told him they had arrived in Woodlake. Apparently they had made it this far without losing any more time.

There was nothing apart from the sign to be seen through the windows and Mick took the opportunity to stretch his legs even though it was still raining very heavily. Two or three other passengers from the other carriages had also taken the opportunity.

Woodlake appeared to consist of two buildings, one on each side of the track but apart from the few passengers hardy enough to brave the elements and the engineer and fireman refuelling the train, there was no sign of life at all, not even a lamp could be seen in either of the buildings. Eventually Mick boarded the train and made his way to the guard's van.

'That dog of yours ain't even closed his eyes,' announced the guard. 'I even offered him somethin' to eat but he just refused to touch it.'

'Damn thing is makin' me nervous,' complained Harold Buck. 'All it's done is stare right at us.'

'I feel real sorry for you,' sneered Mick. He patted the dog which, apparently for the first time since leaving Greenhills, raised its head and wagged its tail. 'Here boy,' said Mick, pointing at some bread and meat in front of it, 'eat it up.' The dog needed no second bidding and quickly ate the food. 'I guess you could do with a run out.' He turned to the guard. 'How much longer are we likely to be here?'

'Ten minutes, no more,' said the guard. 'You need to be quick if you're goin' to let him out. The engineer will give a single blast when he's ready to leave just to get everyone back on board.'

Mick slid the door back and jumped down, calling the dog after him. He appeared only too pleased and obviously needed the break. His prisoners also complained that they needed to relieve themselves and, grudgingly, Mick climbed back and allowed the men to do what they had to do at the open door. The dog needed no lifting back into the wagon, jumping the three foot or so with great agility. Eventually they were once more on their way.

There was no hope of anyone getting any sleep; the train had slowed dramatically and was being buffeted by high winds and on more than one occasion appeared in imminent danger of being blown over. Strangely, the only passenger who appeared completely unconcerned –although she did refer to the wind – was the lone, elderly lady. One of the businessmen was becoming quite hysterical and when a man appeared from the private carriage he demanded to know just what the railroad company were going to do about it. He did not really appreciate the reply that while the president of the company had god-like powers, even he was unable to control the weather.

They had apparently been climbing which, along with the wind, accounted for the reduced speed. Suddenly Mick was aware that they were now travelling down-hill and that their speed was increasing and the train was swaying rather alarmingly. In fact, at that point, even the elderly lady became very concerned.

TWO

It was obvious to both Mick Nelson and the elderly lady that the train was out of control. Loud squeals seemed to indicate that the engineer was doing his best to slow the runaway train but it was also obvious that he was not succeeding. The carriage lurched dangerously and by that time the passenger who had been hysterical before had been joined by the younger woman whose companion was doing his best to comfort her. The other passengers, though ashen-faced, clung grimly to their seats, bracing themselves for what they all knew was about to happen.

When it did happen, it was not as ferocious as Mick had imagined it would be. The carriage lurched to one side, glass and timber shattered and in a matter of seconds everything had ground to a halt and the carriage was on its side. Apart from the two screaming passengers in the first class, other hysterical screams could be heard from further back. In the mêlée, Mick found the elderly woman had landed on top of him and, after pushing her off and making certain that she was not injured, he checked on the other passengers.

The hysterical man appeared uninjured, as did the younger woman, but the man with her had plainly suffered a broken arm. The other lone male passenger proved to be dead. A large shard of glass protruded from his neck and Mick quickly pulled it out and covered the man's face with a coat he found nearby. The bodyguard had suffered a similar fate, the only difference being that this time a long sliver of wood had completely pierced the man's chest. Mick did not attempt to remove it and left the body where it was.

It took about twenty minutes for Mick to help everyone from the wreckage of the carriage and only when he was satisfied that there was nothing more he could do for them did his thoughts turn to the dog and his prisoners. He made his way against the howling wind and driving rain past the other two carriages to the guard's van. He was amazed to discover that it was standing upright, although off the rails. The guard was standing outside obviously wondering just what he should do.

'I'd go and look what's happened to your president if I was you,' suggested Mick. 'It looks like most folk have survived. There's a couple of men dead in the first class but there could be others in the other carriages. I haven't even looked at the first car but it looks to me like that and the first class took the worst of the crash.' The guard said something which was lost on the wind and made his way along to the private car, apparently thankful that someone had told him what to do.

The dog appeared to be none the worse for his experience and had refused to leave his post, still maintaining a watch over the two outlaws. Only when Mick called him out did he, almost reluctantly it appeared, leave his self-appointed position.

'So what happens now, Marshal?' sneered Saul Evans. 'You goin' to keep us chained up in here?'

'You're safe enough for the time being,' said Mick. 'You can stay there while I see what's happened to everyone else. At least you're dry in there, if anythin' the rain is gettin' worse.' As Mick went to see if he could be of any help amongst the other passengers, the dog did not hesitate to leap back into the car and resume its original position opposite the outlaws.

It appeared that of twenty occupants of the carriage next to the guard's van only two had suffered serious injury. One had a shattered leg and another had serious chest injuries and, according to the elderly lady, who seemed to know about such things, was not expected to survive. The second car turned up three with more serious injuries. There was another broken leg and two with chest injuries, although these did not seem as bad as the first serious chest injury. In fact, apart from cuts and bruises and a bit of hysteria amongst the remaining passengers, the only fatalities had occurred in the first-class car and the private car, both of which were more extensively damaged than the other carriages.

The single death in the private car was that of another bodyguard whose head had been almost severed as he had been partly thrown through a window. The president of the railroad company had suffered a cut to his forehead – which he insisted was life-threatening and demanded immediate attention. He did not appear to appreciate it when Mick told him that he had people with far worse injuries to deal with first.

The elderly lady, Mrs Gladys Sommers,

proved that her original matter-of-fact manner was no act as she passed among the injured administering what help she could, even using her own petticoats as makeshift bandages. Very quickly she assumed charge of the situation and certainly put the president of the railroad in his place when it came to priority of treatment.

Three very small children and one nursing mother were transferred to the guard's van, this being the only suitable dry place. Nobody appeared to notice the fact that Saul Evans and Harold Buck were chained.

The engineer and fireman seemed to have escaped unscathed although the locomotive had toppled on to its side. The engineer had already volunteered to walk along the track to a small shack where, he claimed, he would be able to telegraph details of their predicament. In fact he seemed to be the only person with any idea of exactly where they were. However, he returned in less than half an hour with the news that a bridge about half a mile ahead had been taken out and that crossing the swollen river was impossible. The fireman volunteered to try the opposite direction.

In the meantime the canvas over the load on the flat wagon – which had also remained upright – had been removed and erected as shelter. The removal of the canvas had been ordered by Mrs Sommers despite the protests of the railroad president who appeared more concerned that the surrey which had been under the canvas might suffer damage from the elements.

'To hell with the train, its crew and the passengers,' she complained to Mick. 'All he's interested in is that scratch on his head and his damned surrey.'

In fact the president was even more disturbed to discover that the train had been transporting dangerous outlaws and a dog. The discovery was made when he decided that he and his entourage – which consisted of two more bodyguards, two servants and four men who were apparently advisers of one kind or another, should take over the guard's van. This decision proved too much for both Mrs Sommers and Mick and, along with several other passengers, they prevented the removal of the prisoners and the takeover of the car.

'You obviously don't realize who I am,' he said, grandly. 'I happen to own this railroad and...'

'I don't give a damn if you own the whole United States,' replied Mrs Sommers, equally grandly but deliberately so. 'My husband was a senior circuit judge but that doesn't mean I have to have preferential treatment over other passengers. You will have to wait until either myself or Marshal Nelson has decided who goes where. Children and the injured have priority followed by the women.'

A bodyguard drew his pistol and threatened to use it if anyone attempted to stop them commandeering the car. Mick slowly drew his pistol and thrust it under the nose of the bodyguard and suggested that he might like to try. The man gulped and put his gun away. Eventually the president and his party were allowed to sit under the stretched canvas.

'I don't know who gave you and that woman the right to assume command here, but since you have, what are you going to do, Marshal?' demanded the president. 'It is essential that I get out of here, I have a very important meeting to attend.'

'Then maybe you should make sure your trains run to time,' retorted Mick. 'It was five and half hours late leaving Greenhills. If it had been running to time we might not have run into this storm and so avoided the accident.'

'You are missing the point,' muttered the president. 'That meeting cannot go ahead without me. You do realize that I am the president of the railroad company don't you?'

'You've made that plain enough,' said Mick. 'What the hell do you expect me to do? I haven't the faintest idea where we are or how far away from anyone who might be able to get a message through or do something to help.'

'We're about thirty miles from Delano,' said the engineer, who had also taken refuge under the canvas. 'There's no chance of gettin' through though, the bridge is out about half a mile up the track an' nobody can get through, the river's too high.'

'What about the other way?' demanded the president.

'Woodlake is the nearest,' replied the engineer. 'My fireman has gone back to see if we can get through. Even if the bridges are intact, this train ain't goin' nowhere, which means it's goin' to be one hell of a long walk. We're five hours out of Woodlake, five hours train time that is so I reckon it's at least a day's walkin'. There's nothing we can do, anyhow, until he comes back and this storm subsides; at least we do have some form of shelter.'

'And how long will it be before he returns?' demanded the president again.

'That all depends on what he finds,' said the engineer. 'There's four bridges between here and there and anything could have happened.'

'So it looks like you're stuck here with the rest of us,' said Mick. 'Your meeting will just have to wait until you get through.'

'What about those prisoners?' asked one of the president's entourage. 'They should never have been allowed on board. They could be a danger to the president's safety. Serious questions must be asked when this is all over.'

'Not my problem,' replied Mick. 'I was just doin' what I was told.'

'You just make sure they don't escape,' said the man. 'If they do and attack the president you will have serious questions to answer.'

'I'm really worried,' sneered Mick.

Once the injured had been tended to, things started to settle down, most of the passengers trying to snatch some sleep before dawn which, according to Mick's watch, would be about another three hours.

Much to the dismay of the president,

35

curtains which had been at the windows of the private car and the first class had been brought out to be used as makeshift blankets, although there were not enough to go round and even he was refused one on the grounds that there were many more needy cases. The guard's van was also raided in an attempt to find other suitable material to use as blankets and a bolt of cloth was found which was ripped into suitable lengths. Again the president complained that this was misuse of property entrusted to the railroad. He was not quite so vociferous when several boxes of whiskey were discovered and passed amongst the survivors. By that time the rain had ceased and the wind had subsided considerably.

A large fire was lit, using firewood from the tender and timbers from the wreckage and even the president appeared to appreciate the warmth. The dog also took the opportunity to curl up under the wagon, soaking up the heat. The children were complaining of hunger and Mick remembered the bread and butter he had bought in Greenhills. After a search of the wrecked carriage he eventually found them and divided the loaf between the children.

Shortly before dawn the fireman returned

and announced that it was impossible to get through the way they had come. A bridge across a deep ravine had been destroyed. This news immediately brought a new round of demands from the president that Deputy Marshal Mick Nelson must do something. Mick simply ignored the president.

Shortly after dawn Mick was compelled to allow his prisoners out of the guard's van to attend to the call of nature. This would not normally have presented any problems but on this occasion the member of the president's entourage who had earlier threatened to use his gun decided to accompany Mick and the two outlaws into the forest. He claimed this was in the interests of the president's safety.

He walked alongside Harold Buck, making certain that both outlaws could see the pistol at his side. He obviously intended his action to show that he was prepared to use the gun should they attempt to do anything. Mick did point out that, shackled as they were, they certainly would not get very far if they decided to make a break for it. This fact seemed lost on the man.

Suddenly a young girl appeared from behind a bush and, for no apparent reason, the bodyguard pushed her roughly to one side, in fact pushing her into the path of Harold Buck who, it appeared, acted perfectly normally in grabbing the girl to prevent her falling. However, he was plainly a very quick thinker and at the same time, unseen by Mick, had snatched the pistol from the bodyguard's belt. Apparently using the fact that his wrists were manacled to disguise his clumsy actions, he twisted himself and the girl round to face Mick Nelson, the pistol now firmly dug into the girl's temple and the chain between his wrists firmly across her throat. Mick's first reaction was to go for his own gun but the bodyguard chose that moment to place himself between Mick and Harold Buck.

'Don't even think of it, Marshal,' warned Buck. 'I ain't got nothin' to lose, I'm for the hangman's rope anyhow so killin' this girl ain't goin' to make no difference.' The girl was obviously too terrified to even scream, all she could do was to stare wide-eyed and pleadingly at Mick.

'Kill her an' you're dead meat for sure,' grated Mick, his hand resting on the handle of his revolver but not actually drawing it.

'She'll be fine just so long as you do what I say,' rasped Buck. 'First you hand over your gun an' gunbelt to Saul, then you unlock these damned shackles. You too,' he said to the bodyguard. 'We'll take the belt of yours as well.'

'Best do as he says,' croaked the bodyguard, already starting to remove the belt which had about twenty bullets round it. He was obviously terrified that he might be shot.

'I'll decide what's best,' growled Mick. 'This wouldn't've happened but for you taggin' along. No deal, Buck. If you want to die it'll sure save me a lot of time and bother.'

'Like Harold says, Marshal,' said Saul Evans, 'We're both due for the rope so you killin' us out here might even be a blessin'. OK, so it might suit you but how are you goin' to explain to your bosses what happened to the girl. More importantly, how are you goin' to convince her mother that she had to die? Believe me, he'll shoot her an' think nothin' of it if you force him.'

Mick was well aware of the reputation of both men. In fact one of the murders they were implicated in was the rape and murder of a girl not much older than this girl seemed to be and he knew that he had little option but to do as they demanded.

By that time the bodyguard had removed his gunbelt and handed it to Saul Evans, suggesting that since he had done as he was told he should be allowed to leave. Saul Evans simply laughed and sneered and ordered the man to drop to his knees, which he did, pleading for mercy. When Mick eventually handed over his belt and gun Evans slowly drew the pistol and levelled it at the bodyguard's head. This brought more sobbings and pleadings.

'Please,' croaked the bodyguard, 'I don't want to die. I've done nothing to you, please don't kill me.'

'Leave it, Saul,' ordered Buck. 'You'll only attract other folk. Get those keys an' get these shackles off.'

'C'mon, Marshal,' said Evans. 'The keys! We want these things off.'

'Let the girl go,' said Mick.

'No deal,' rasped Buck. 'She gets to go free once you've taken these things off an' not before.'

'Do as he says,' pleaded the bodyguard. 'I don't want to die.'

Mick realized that he had very little option but to release the outlaws, being quite sure that they would certainly carry out their threat. He produced a bunch of four keys and unlocked the shackles on Saul Evans and then those on Harold Buck.

'Now,' sneered Evans, 'just to make sure you don't follow us too soon, we're goin' to shackle you both to a tree. You,' he said to Mick, 'stand up facin' that tree.' He indicated one of the smaller trees. Mick did as he was told. 'Now put your arms round the trunk.' Again Mick complied with the order. 'Now you can see what it feels like to be manacled.' The wrist manacles were clipped shut around his wrists and locked. The bodyguard was also chained to another tree in the same way. Much to Mick's horror, the keys were then thrown as far as Evans could throw them into the forest.

'What about the girl?' asked Mick. 'Let her go.'

'She's our insurance,' said Buck. 'She gets to go free once we're far enough away from here. You just remember that, Marshal. I know for sure you'll be comin' after us, but when you do, just think of what might happen to her.' The girl seemed too terrified to do anything, even to cry as she was led away deeper into the forest.

'Now what are you goin' to do, Marshal?' demanded the bodyguard, his belligerence and confidence suddenly returning. 'You should never have brought those outlaws on this train.'

'And if you'd stayed to mind your president instead of interferin' this would never have happened,' retorted Mick. 'Right now you can prove you might be of some use an' start hollerin' for help.'

Both men started shouting.

It appeared that it had been the dog who had first heard the calls for help and had rushed off into the forest, quickly finding Mick. Mick ordered the animal to go and find Mrs Sommers and get her or anyone else to come and rescue them. The dog seemed to understand and raced back to the train where he grabbed a hold of Mrs Sommer's dress and tugged.

'What in the name of goodness has got into you?' she scolded. The dog released her dress and yapped before taking a few quick steps towards the forest, stopping to see if she was following.

'Looks like he wants you to follow him,' observed a young man. 'Doesn't he belong to the marshal?'

'You're right,' she said, 'he does want me to follow. Something must have happened to the marshal. Come along, young man, I might need some help.'

Finding Mick and the bodyguard was the easy part, releasing them a totally different matter. Although a brief search for the keys was made it was too dark and the undergrowth too dense. Mrs Sommers enlisted the help of several other men and eventually a large axe was brought from the guard's van and the suggestion made that someone try and cut through the chains. This idea certainly did not appeal to Mick since the chain between each wrist was no more than eight inches and just one wild swing even by an experienced axeman would almost certainly lead to the loss of one hand. It was finally agreed that the trees would have to be chopped down.

This involved Mick and the bodyguard lying on the ground whilst two men took it in turns to cut down the trees. Fortunately, being fairly small trees, the operation did not take too long, even though there was not a lot of space to work. Eventually both men were free of the trees if not the manacles.

Mick's first thought was for the mother of the girl who had been kidnapped and he expected her to break down in hysterics when told. In fact she maintained her composure remarkably well, assuring Mick that she did not blame him at all. The bodyguard on the other hand blamed Mick for everything, telling everyone that had it not been for the marshal's cowardice it would never have happened and that he, James Bennet, had been prepared to shoot the men but had been prevented from doing so. Mick listened in disbelief and vowed that he would make the bodyguard eat his words at the first opportunity. He did not waste his time trying to contradict the man at that point. Mrs Sommers and most of the others made it plain that they did not believe the bodyguard's account.

It was suggested that the only way to at least free their hands was to cut the chain using the axe. Once again Mick was not too happy with the idea when suddenly a small, elderly, wiry man appeared and announced that lock had not yet been made that he could not unfasten. After looking almost casually at the manacles he produced two stout pieces of wire from a leather pouch and, in less than ten seconds Mick was free. He felt like suggesting that James Bennet, the bodyguard, should remain shackled but in another few seconds he too was free.

'I need a gun and some ammunition,' said Mick. 'I have to go after them.'

'I think it is your duty to remain here,' said the railroad president. 'We are far more important than one girl or two outlaws. They will probably be captured again later.'

'Yeh, after they've killed the girl!' snarled Mick. 'There's nothin' I can do here, all you can do is wait for help to arrive. Anyhow, it could be that I will be able to get a message through somehow. Men like you make me sick. You think you are so damned important...' Mrs Sommers touched his arm and quietened him down.

Eventually a belt, pistol and fifty rounds of ammunition were provided by one of the younger men, who also volunteered to accompany Mick. Mick refused the offer with grateful thanks, saying that he preferred to work alone. The thin, wiry lock-picker also produced a rifle and a box of twenty bullets, warning Mick that the gun had not been used for at least three years and that it had belonged to the man's son. It appeared that the son was dead.

'Look after the dog,' Mick said to Mrs Sommers as he was about to leave. 'When you get out of here you can send a message through to the governor's office tellin' me where he is.'

Mrs Sommers laughed and pointed at the

dog now quickly heading into the forest. 'I'd say that you are not going anywhere without him,' she said. 'I think he understood what you were saying.'

THREE

Before he set out to follow the outlaws and the girl, Mick made quite certain that everything that could be done for the survivors of the crash was being done and that there was really no need for him to remain. Mrs Sommers assured him that she and one or two of the others could deal with any problems which might arise and that it was his duty to try and rescue the girl.

He had established the girl's name as Mary Brennan, that she was twelve years old, that she was the eldest of four and that she and her mother were on their way back home, where the other three children had been left with a relative. It appeared that Mrs Brennan's husband had died some twelve months previously. Although obviously very worried about the fate of her daughter, Mrs Brennan retained her composure and did not appear to hold anyone responsible for what had happened. Satisfied that there was nothing else he could do, Mick started out after the outlaws.

At first there was no sign of the dog which had taken to the forest and although he called and whistled, it was not until Mick was about a mile away from the railroad that he suddenly found it trotting alongside him as if it had never been away. He said something about sending him back but realized that it would be a waste of time and, patting the animal, told him that everything was all right.

'OK,' he said to the dog, 'you've got yourself a job. You can help me find the girl. She's more important than those men, you just remember that.' The dog wagged his tail as if understanding every word. Mick was quite prepared to believe that this was the case.

Following the outlaws' trail through the forest was very easy. They had apparently made no attempt to cover their tracks, obviously intent on putting as much distance between Mick and themselves as possible. They had a start of almost one and a half hours and, although having the encumbrance of the girl, it appeared that they were making very good headway since even Mick's limited tracking ability told him that he did not appear to be gaining on them.

Although the tracks left by the outlaws

seemed obvious, he was occasionally thrown into confusion since there were also many animal tracks and runs criss-crossing the trail. On two occasions Mick came across signs which seemed to indicate that his quarry had gone in a certain direction and was prepared to follow the new trail. However, on each occasion the dog barked at him and insisted on following a different trail. When, on the second occasion they came across a piece of material snagged on a thorn bush, which looked as though if could have come from the girl's dress, Mick was forced to concede that the animal probably knew better than he did. He kept the material to allow the dog to sniff it and hopefully pick up the girl's scent. Thereafter, if there was ever any question of which way to go, he allowed the dog to make the decision.

At about four o'clock in the afternoon the dog became quite agitated and shortly afterwards they came across a small log cabin set in a clearing. For a while Mick studied the cabin from the safety of the trees just in case the outlaws should have chosen to hide up there.

After a time he was reasonably certain that there was nobody in the cabin, but at the same time he was wary since the dog appeared to think differently; although he was not actually barking he whined and was still agitated. Mick cautiously approached the cabin, kicked open the door and stood to one side, fully expecting a volley of shots, but nothing happened.

The dog was first in, whimpering slightly and when Mick followed he saw a body in the middle of the mud floor. A quick examination showed that it was the body of a man and that he was dead, apparently shot since there was a gaping wound in his temple.

He had to assume that the man was a fur trapper judging by his attire, his full beard, the various vicious-looking traps which adorned the walls and a large pile of furs along one side of the cabin. The stench from the furs was almost overpowering and Mick had to get some fresh air. The dog, on the other hand, seemed to find the smell very interesting.

The fact that the blood around the wound, although swarming with flies, was still slightly tacky, indicated that the trapper had been killed fairly recently and appeared to confirm that Harold Buck and Saul Evans had passed that way. He could think of no reason why they should have murdered the trapper, but it seemed plain that they had done so even if the motive was not apparent.

One possible reason for the murder suddenly struck Mick as he was making an examination of the cabin in an attempt to discover the identity of the man. If he made it through he would have to report the death for the record if nothing else, although it was not unknown for such men never to be identified since, as often as not, there was no record of them having ever existed. He suddenly realized that every trapper or hunter he had ever met – and he had met a few – always carried a rifle, or at least a shotgun, but there was neither rifle nor shotgun, to be found, although he did discover a box of bullets which seemed to confirm that a rifle was involved.

The trapper's identity remained a mystery; there was absolutely nothing amongst what few personal papers the man had possessed which gave any clues at all. The only thing which, Mick decided, might help to identify the man was a receipt for furs dated some three months earlier from a trading company in somewhere called Overton. Mick had no idea where Overton was or even if it was a town or simply a trading post. He put all the personal papers in his pocket.

By the time he had buried the man – which seemed to be the decent thing to do – dusk was drawing in and he decided to remain in the cabin for the night. He had, by that time, become hardened to the smell of the furs.

Food presented no problem; hanging over the recessed fireplace were a number of dried, smoked meats, although Mick had no idea just what they were. However, they were plainly cured for the purpose of eating and he eventually selected something which, he thought, looked like deer meat. There were a few strange-looking vegetables in a basket and a small stream close to the cabin appeared to be the main source of water. In a matter of an hour Mick had cooked himself a rather tasty meal. The dog was obviously very happy to eat nothing but meat.

The following morning was in stark contrast to the previous few days. The sky, what he could see of it through the leaf canopy, appeared to be cloudless and it promised to be a hot day. It seemed that the flies and midges had also been awakened by the sun, although the flies had been well in evidence the previous day. The flies lost no time in invading the pile of furs, definitely seeming to prefer them to the meat hanging above the fire. Mick found a small hessian sack into which he dropped two of the larger dried pieces of some animal or animals to save him having to hunt for food later that day. The only other thing he did was to take a small tin cooking-pot, a well used billycan and a supply of coffee with him.

Unlike the flies, the midges seemed to prefer a diet of human meat, apparently leaving the dog alone but swarming around all Mick's exposed parts and no amount of arm waving made the slightest difference to their relentless onslaught. In fact the more he tried to ward them off the worse they seemed to get. He had heard that midges did not like the leaves from certain plants when rubbed on the skin, but not having any idea which leaves or plants to use he did not bother to try any. Eventually he learned to tolerate the midges, although his face and neck in particular ended up a mass of red itchy bites which, he soon discovered, were made more painful by scratching.

At mid-morning the trees became sparser

and eventually disappeared almost completely as they came out on to a wide, flat valley across which flowed what appeared to be a series of shallow rivers. Mick realized that they were all actually part of the same river spreading across the plain. Crossing the valley and having to negotiate the many streams meant that he lost all sight of any trail the outlaws might have left. However, up to that point he had been reasonably certain that he had still been following them, primarily because there did not appear to be any other way they could have gone and the dog also appeared to think that they were still on the right trail.

To give himself some respite from the midges, Mick lay down in one of the streams and allowed the surprisingly cold water to wash over him. The dog confined his activity to simply drinking the water and looking at Mick as though he had taken leave of his senses.

Once he had crossed the streams and reached slightly higher ground, picking up the trail again proved impossible. There were so many tracks, most of which had obviously been created by animals coming down to the water, that finding the one the outlaws had chosen would have been a matter of pure luck. Even the dog seemed unable to pick up their scent.

At that point, although Evans and Buck had been heading steadily eastward, Mick wondered if they might have chosen to follow the river downstream. He could not imagine either of them being prepared to spend the remainder of their days living in such a remote area as this. They were hardened outlaws and one thing he had learned, even in his fairly short time as a deputy marshal, was that the vast majority of outlaws needed to be around other people.

He looked up at the mountains which, at that point, appeared to rise almost vertically and were capped in snow, and decided that he was going to take a chance on the outlaws having headed south down what seemed the easier route.

Two hours later, as they were passing through an area of thick bush, the dog suddenly stopped, its hackles raised and gave a very low, throaty growl. Mick immediately cocked the rather ancient rifle he had been given and moved slowly forward. The dog remained protectively at his heels, hackles still raised and a constant rumble in his throat. The reason for the dog's action suddenly became frighteningly clear.

There was a loud roar followed by something obviously very large crashing through the bushes, apparently straight towards Mick and the dog. There was no mistaking the fact that it was a bear and that it was making its presence felt in an attempt to scare off what it considered intruders. Mick stood his ground, rifle at the ready and waited.

The bear, an enormous grizzly, suddenly appeared in front of them, no more than ten yards away, stopping as it eyed the intruders, rocking from side to side on all fours and growling at them before rearing on to its hind legs, its huge arms spread wide and showing very large and plainly very sharp claws. Mick held his fire; he had tried shooting a bear once before and knew that it was not as easy as it might seem. The bear he had been forced to shoot at before had hardly seemed to notice the bullet and he had heard other men say the same.

Suddenly the dog was rushing towards the huge animal, expertly avoiding the flailing claws and gnashing teeth, nipping the bear on the leg and then dashing away. The bear seemed to lose interest in Mick and turned its attention to the yapping dog and bellowed with rage. Once again the dog raced in dangerously close, again managing to avoid the claws and teeth and then running off. This was repeated another three times, all the time the bear being lured further and further away from Mick.

Eventually Mick lost sight of both grizzly and dog, the only indication as to where they were being the yaps and roars of both animals. All went quiet for a few moments and Mick feared for the life of the dog but suddenly he was back at his side, wagging his tail and looking very pleased with himself. As the bush thinned out Mick caught sight of the huge grizzly lumbering across the shallow river.

'Thanks, feller,' said Mick, patting the dog. 'I don't know what I'd've done if you hadn't been here. Now, we have to find that girl.' He took the piece of material from his pocket and allowed the dog to sniff it.

Some time later, a dull roar some distance ahead told Mick that they were approaching either a waterfall or a set of rapids. It proved to be the former. The river suddenly dropped vertically for what looked like 300 or 400 feet. From there the water was forced through a narrow canyon in a series of angry-looking rapids and any suggestion of him or anyone else also going through the canyon was completely out of the question.

Nor was there any question of climbing down the sheer cliff which formed the waterfall and stretched right round to the canyon, making it impossible to follow the top of the canyon. The only way through appeared to involve a climb towards what seemed to be a narrow pass high above the canyon. Having come this far and by no means certain that he was still following the outlaws, Mick felt that he had no alternative but to continue.

Mick never actually heard anything, nor did he really feel anything. When he came to all he was aware of was a dull ache in his head, the dog licking his face and whimpering at him. He felt his head and found a deep, painful crease across his scalp, the blood having congealed into his hair which made him think that he must have been lying unconscious for some considerable time.

It was still daylight but there was something about the position of the sun which did not seem quite right. It was not until he had washed the dried blood out of his hair and studied the bullet hole in his hat that he realized just what was wrong with the sun.

It was a morning sun, whereas it ought to have been an afternoon sun. He realized that he had just spent at least one night completely unconscious perhaps more for all he knew. He glanced at his pocket watch but it had stopped, indicating a time of four minutes past eight.

While he now realized that he had been unconscious for some considerable time, what he did not know was that the dog had, apart from one short period, remained constantly at his side and had even warned off a large, curious moose. He had not even attempted to eat any of the meat in the hessian sack which lay nearby, now the object of interest to a large number of ants. Mick groggily picked up the sack and washed it and the meat in the river. He realized that he was certainly in no condition to start hunting for food. It was at that moment that he realized both his rifle and pistol and gunbelt were missing, which made any thought of hunting purely academic.

Painful as his experience had been, it did at least confirm that he was on the right trail, although just how far Buck and Evans were now ahead was an unknown factor. He now also knew for certain that they were in possession of at least two rifles and three pistols.

The fact that his guns and ammunition were missing told him that Buck and Evans must have checked on the accuracy of their shot and he had to assume that the quantity of blood had convinced them that he was dead. There was simply no other explanation.

At that moment Mick was in no condition to resume his search or worry too much about having lost his guns. He decided to allow himself a few hours to recover in the shade of some trees. He and the dog ate one of the pieces of smoked meat after which Mick closed his eyes for a few minutes.

He awoke with a start and suddenly realized that he was quite cold and that it was dark. His few minutes of sleep had turned into a few hours, exactly how many was a mystery. He had absolutely no idea what time it was since telling the time by the moon was not one of his skills although he had heard tales of some bushmen and Indians having that ability. The dog obviously sensed that he was awake and gently nuzzled his chest.

'Looks like I made a real hash of things,' he said, stroking the animal. 'I must have lost at least two days, they could be any-where by now.' There was plainly no point in starting out in the dark and once again he settled down to await the coming of dawn. 'You just let me know when it's daylight,' he instructed the dog.

He had been joking when he had told the animal to wake him at dawn and nobody could have been more surprised than he when, just as the first rays of the morning were creeping over the distant mountains, the dog scratched at his arm and barked in his ear.

They ate the remaining meat and then started on their way, Mick feeling much better. The dog seemed to pick up the scent of the outlaws shortly afterwards which did not come as any surprise. It appeared that they too had headed for the high pass above the canyon.

Saul Evans and Harold Buck studied the small community from what they had considered to be a safe distance, although judging by the actions of the people in the community, it appeared that they had been seen. Some men were in the process of arming themselves and pointing to where Buck, Evans and the girl were hiding.

'What do you reckon?' asked Evans. 'They know we're here an' they don't seem too friendly.'

'Well without us makin' one hell of a detour,' replied Buck, 'we ain't got much alternative but to go through. Maybe they ain't as unfriendly as they look. Hell, they can't get many strangers passin' through up here so I guess it's only natural they should be wary.'

'OK,' agreed Evans, 'we go through. Maybe we can get some decent food off 'em. Just keep your hand on your gun, just in case, though.'

They made their way slowly along the rutted track down the hill towards the community and at the same time several men formed a line between the outlaws and the first building, each man holding his rifle threateningly. When the outlaws were about twenty yards away an order was barked by the defenders. Although the man had spoken in what, to Evans and Buck, was a foreign language, the meaning of the order needed no translating. When they had stopped, the man who had first spoken stepped forward a few yards and, again in the foreign tongue, asked another question. Once again, the question required little in the way of interpretation but Harold Buck acted as though he had no idea what was being said.

'Don't you speak English?' he asked.

'We choose not to speak English,' replied the man, plainly the leader of the community. 'We are not English. Since you do not speak our language and I am one of the few here who do speak English, I will address you in English. I asked what you were doing here?'

'Just passin' through,' replied Buck. 'Ain't no law about passin' through as far as I know.'

'We have been here for many years,' said the man. 'People do not normally pass through, as you put it, from the direction you have come. There are a few fur trappers who do but they are known to us and we do not see them very often. I ask again, what are you doing here?'

'Mindin' our own business,' said Evans, 'just like you should be doin'. We ain't done you no harm an' we don't intend to. Now if you was at all friendly you'd be offerin' us some food an' possibly shelter for the night.'

'You have the look of gunmen,' said the man, smiling slightly. He turned and spoke to the others and there seemed to be a general consensus of opinion although it was plain that Mary Brennan was a topic of interest. The line parted to allow Buck, Evans and the girl through.

'You are right,' said the leader, 'it is none of our business and you are most welcome to share our food. As for shelter, the best we can offer is some dry hay in a barn.'

'That's better,' said Buck. 'Thanks, we will stay the night if we can. Where is the nearest town?'

The man repeated the question in his own language to the others and they all laughed. 'That is a town called Lindsay, but it is at least two more days away even riding a horse or a mule. Walking it will take three or four days. Come, you must be very tired. Food is being prepared and will be brought to you. In the meantime you must make yourselves comfortable in the barn...' He indicated a largish wooden structure behind what appeared to be two houses. 'It is not fitting that the girl stay with you. She will stay with my family in the house.' Both Buck and Evans were about to protest but then decided against it.

'What say we leave her here,' suggested Evans when they were settled in the barn. 'We don't need her no more, she's only slowin' us down.'

'Maybe we could,' agreed Harold Buck. 'They might not want her to stay here though.'

'Then we just leave her,' said Saul Evans. 'We just make sure we're out of here before dawn.'

For her part, Mary Brennan was even more terrified of the young men who flocked round to leer at her. The women tried talking to her in a strange language, some feeling her long, blonde hair and laughing. There did not appear to be any young women or girls about and what were obviously coarse comments constantly passed between the women and two young men in particular.

The man who appeared to be the village elder did not make any attempt to communicate with her other than to tell her to sit at the table where the food was being served. Buck and Evans were also brought from the barn.

It was plain that mealtimes were taken in complete silence other than for grace to be said before they actually started to eat. After the meal Mary Brennan was given a brief order to clear away the dishes and to wash up. Buck and Evans, though surprised, said nothing and Mary meekly did as she was told. It was not until the elder and the two outlaws were sitting on the porch outside the house that the elder spoke.

'It seems obvious to me that you are running from the law,' he suddenly said. He was not so much asking but making a statement of fact. 'I do not know what the girl is to you but I suspect that you are holding her as hostage. You will leave her here, I will even buy her from you.' Both Evans and Buck looked startled. 'That is correct,' said the elder. 'You heard me correctly, you will sell me the girl.'

'Sell!' exclaimed Buck. 'Oh, oh yeh, I see what you mean, at least I think I do.'

'I suspect that you do not understand,' said the elder, smiling knowingly. 'It might not have escaped your notice that we do not have any young women here. Unfortunately we have been cursed with an over-abundance of boys and, as is the natural order of things, young men eventually grow up to need young women. Indeed it is essential for the survival of our community. I am offering to buy the girl from you. We are a very remote people, in fact few know of our existence and even fewer would care. There would certainly be nobody looking for her up here and even if someone did come I can assure you that they would never find her. In time she will learn to accept us and our way of life, especially when she is given as wife to one of our young men. I could, of course, arrange to have you killed and simply take her. I can assure you that your bodies would never be found either and it is certain that nobody would come looking for either of you. However, we are a peaceful community and wish no harm on anyone.'

'And if we refuse?' asked Buck. 'Don't answer that, I already know, our bodies would never be found.'

'You learn fast,' nodded the elder. 'How much do you want for her?'

FOUR

Although there was plenty of game just for the taking, Mick's one problem was that without a rifle or even a pistol, he had no means of taking it. He had even tried spearing fish but had failed dismally, although when he had seen even small boys doing it it had looked so easy. He had eventually resigned himself to eating what few berries were available or going hungry and, since what berries he did find were mostly unripe, it appeared that he would have to go hungry. However, the dog once again came to the rescue as it suddenly raced off after a large rabbit which they had disturbed. The rabbit was fast but the dog was even faster.

For the first time the dog showed some sign of selfishness in that it was very reluctant to part with its catch. It took Mick some time to persuade it to loosen its vice-like grip and it even growled threateningly. Eventually he managed to persuade it to part with the rabbit and, using a knife he had found in the trapper's cabin, gutted, skinned it and, using some matches he had also found in the cabin, cooked it over an open fire using the utensils he had taken from the cabin. The dog was happy to eat all the offal raw but appeared to appreciate the cooked meat as well. Mick made himself some coffee, the first he had had since tasting Mrs Spencer's at Greenhills. He was uncertain if his tasted any better than hers.

For two full days he and the dog had followed what he assumed must be the trail of the outlaws. He constantly reminded the dog of the girl's scent by showing it the piece of cloth and the dog always responded by wagging his tail and racing off ahead, his nose firmly sniffing the ground.

Shortly before midday on the third day the dog started to act strangely and suddenly disappeared into the brush. Mick did not actually see which way it went, he was only aware that it was no longer at his feet. However, he did not worry about it, knowing that it was probably far better suited to look after itself than he was and that it would return when it was good and ready.

A gruff voice, barking what he assumed to be an order, came from somewhere behind him. The click of a gun being cocked warned him not to turn round too fast and to raise his hands slightly to indicate that he was unarmed. The gruff voice said something else in a language Mick could not understand and he slowly turned to face an ancient-looking muzzle-loading rifle held by an equally ancient-looking, bearded man. Mick made certain that his badge of office was very visible but this seemed to go unnoticed by the man.

'Put that thing down,' ordered Mick. 'It might go off an' hurt somebody an' I don't want that somebody to be me.' The man responded by again growling something which Mick did not understand and then making waving motions with the rifle. Mick assumed this meant that he was to walk on ahead.

Quite suddenly and totally unexpected by either of them, a fairly small bundle of black and white launched itself from under a nearby bush and landed squarely on the old man's chest. The rifle exploded but the shot went harmlessly into the air. The old man was forced to the ground by the impact of the dog and in an instant Mick had wrestled the gun from the man and had drawn a large knife from the man's belt and was holding it to his throat.

'Now what was that you were sayin'?' demanded Mick. He patted his deputy's badge. 'Deputy Marshal Mick Nelson,' he said, loudly. 'An' I don't like folk pointin' any guns at me.' The man again said something Mick could not understand. 'Speak English!' he ordered. The man shook his head and said something else Mick did not understand. 'I said, speak English,' he repeated. A low growl from the dog told Mick that he and the old man were not alone. He did not turn round but pressed the knife a little harder against the old man's throat, drawing some blood. 'He dies first,' he called back.

'He does not speak English,' said a voice. 'There are few of us here who do. Please, allow him to get up, he is an old man, the oldest in the community. Anyway, I would doubt if you could kill him before I shot you.' Mick turned to see a tall, thin man holding a rifle. 'Please, do as I say, I do not wish to shoot you.' Mick sighed and obeyed and the dog suddenly disappeared amongst the bushes again.

'You shouldn't allow old men an' very small children to handle guns,' he said as he released the man and stood up. 'Deputy Marshal Mick Nelson,' he said, accentuating the word marshal. 'It wouldn't do to kill a marshal.' The man nodded and lowered the rifle. 'OK, so now we've got that sorted out, just who the hell are you and, more importantly, where the hell am I?'

'To take your questions in order of apparent importance,' replied the man in perfect English. 'You are near the community of Wuppertal, not that that would mean much to you. We are a small community of Germans who live out here in an effort to retain our traditional way of life. The nearest town which might mean something to you is Lindsay and that is at least another three days' walking from here, possibly four. The answer to your first question I have partly answered, but my name is Gerhart Schneider.'

'Lindsay I know about,' said Mick. 'I ain't never heard of you lot before though. I've heard about folk like you who come over here from Europe but don't want to change your way of life. Personally I don't see the point in comin' here if you want things to stay the same. Things out here aren't the same.'

'Unfortunately what you say is very true,' replied the man. 'We all know that change must come but we want to give ourselves time to embrace it. However, might I ask what brings a deputy marshal out here, especially coming from the direction you have? I see also that you do not carry a gun. I would have thought that a gun was essential in your work.'

'It's a long story,' said Mick. 'All you need to know is that I'm on the trail of two outlaws and a twelve-year-old girl.' He removed his hat and bent his head slightly to show the man the cut on his head. 'As for my guns, they must've thought they'd killed me. After they shot me they took my pistol an' my rifle an' left me for dead.'

'You must allow us to tend that wound,' said the man, peering closely at it. 'It does not look very healthy to me. Come, my house is not far away. My wife is very good at cleaning and dressing wounds.' He spoke in German to the old man who nodded solemnly and marched off at a surprisingly fast pace.

'Have you seen two men and a girl?' asked Mick. 'I reckon they must've passed through here somethin' like two days ago at least, maybe more. I must admit that I've lost all track of time.'

'We have seen nobody,' said Schneider. 'Apart from the occasional hunter or fur trapper and sometimes a few Indians, we rarely see anyone.'

'They must have come this way,' said Mick. 'There just isn't any other way they could've gone. Anyhow, my dog seems pretty certain they did come this way and he ain't been wrong yet.'

'Even dogs can be wrong,' said Schneider, smiling. 'We do not have any dogs, we have no need for them and we do not believe in keeping animals unless they are working animals or can be used as food. I can assure you that we have seen nobody for at least two weeks until you came along.'

Mick had the feeling that the dog had probably made the wisest move in disappearing. He could not put a finger on it but his gut feeling was that things were not as they seemed. He did not attempt to call the dog.

It looked as if the entire community had assembled to stare at Mick and an elderly lady insisted on attending to his injury. He did not mind that and she appeared very thorough, although his questions went unanswered or received a grin and a nod of the head. Eventually she was satisfied and he was offered a seat at a table where hot food suddenly appeared. Gerhart Schneider joined him although he did not eat.

'I have asked everyone if they have seen two men and a girl,' he said. 'Like me, they are all quite certain that no such people have passed this way in recent times and certainly not a young girl. I am sorry we cannot be of any help.'

'Me too,' sighed Mick. Once again the feeling that all was not as it seemed came over him. 'Thanks for the food an' cleanin' up my head,' he said. 'I've lost enough time as it is, I'll be on my way.'

'I hope that you find the girl,' said Schneider. 'Her mother must be very worried.' The elderly lady who had attended to his wound insisted on giving him a large cloth in which there was some food. 'It is not much,' continued Schneider, 'some bread and some cheese, but it will save you from going hungry for a while.' Mick was actually most grateful and thanked the woman.

A short time later he was on his way but it was not long before he had the distinct feeling that he was being followed. He had to assume that, for reasons known only to them, they were making certain that he did leave. This added to his feeling that all was not as it appeared on the surface, but not having anything definite to act on, certainly there was no hint of anything illegal, and since finding the girl was his priority, he had to accept the fact that perhaps they were being a little too cautious or that he was being too sensitive.

However, the feeling that he was being followed persisted for over an hour, during which time there was no sign of the dog. Once again he did not worry about this since he knew that it would turn up when good and ready.

At almost the same instant that he sensed that his follower had given up, the dog was suddenly at his side. This time, however, he seemed very agitated and kept stopping, whimpering and making little runs back in the direction they had come. By this time Mick had learned to accept the fact that sometimes the dog knew something he did not, besides which its behaviour accentuated his own feeling that something was very wrong back at the German community.

'OK, feller,' he said, 'this time I'm with you.' He started to walk back towards the community. 'You go on ahead an' see if there's anyone about, we don't want to warn 'em.' He pointed ahead and the dog immediately raced off.

Twice the dog came back, each time turning and growling, a signal which Mick read as meaning that somebody was ahead. On each occasion both he and the dog hid among the bushes and each time someone appeared.

The first was a young man carrying a shotgun who seemed to be hunting for squirrels, firing at one but missing. Whether or not the youth was actually hunting or simply gaining some shooting practice was unclear, but he eventually turned back towards the community. On the second occasion a middle-aged woman appeared and was obviously gathering mushrooms and other edible fungi. She too eventually disappeared in the direction of the community.

Mick was quite pleased with this activity since it seemed to indicate that they had lowered their guard and had assumed that he had continued walking towards Lindsay. If this was the case they would not be expecting him. Being unarmed, Mick knew that the element of surprise was going to play a large part in whatever happened next, if, indeed, anything was going to happen. His gut feeling was that Gerhart Schneider had known far more about Saul Evans, Harold Buck and Mary Brennan than he was prepared to admit although neither he nor anyone else in the community had given the slightest indication otherwise.

Eventually Mick was overlooking the community from the safe cover of some thick bush on the edge of the forest and at first everything appeared perfectly normal. However, the dog had chosen that moment to desert him again and it eventually showed itself, seen only by Mick, behind what seemed to be a small barn, racing along the length of it and then eventually stopping to sniff at the boards and then wag its tail furiously.

Normally Mick would have assumed that the object of the dog's interest was another dog, probably a bitch on heat, but Schneider had told him that they did not keep any dogs and he had no reason to disbelieve him. There had certainly been no indication of any domestic animals other than a small herd of milk cows roaming freely close to the community. It was therefore quite plain that the dog's interest was in something or someone else. Without thinking, his hand touched the piece of material in his pocket and it suddenly dawned on him just what the dog might have found.

The dog had disappeared again, obviously

sensing that someone was walking round to the back of the barn. A young man appeared carrying what was plainly a rifle and not the usual shotgun. He seemed to be acting as some sort of guard. Suddenly the dog was at Mick's side, furiously wagging its tail.

'I get the message, feller,' said Mick, patting the animal. 'You're tryin' to tell me that she's in there. What about Evans an' Buck though?' He did not get any further response from the dog. 'Just the girl?' he continued. 'Now why should Schneider lie about not havin' seen her?'

He was now reasonably satisfied that Mary Brennan was in the community and being detained against her will. The question whether or not Evans and Buck were also there remained unanswered for the moment. His problem was exactly how he was going to rescue the girl.

If he had been armed there would have been no problem but, having once in the past had to deal with a similar situation, he also knew that such isolated communities were quite capable of committing murder in order to preserve their way of life.

On that occasion he had had to rescue a woman and her son, the woman having decided to leave the community. She had been abducted and forcibly returned to the man who claimed to be her husband and father of her son. He had had to shoot his way out of that situation in the end, although he had rescued the boy and his mother. Exactly how this related to Mary Brennan was still something of a mystery.

The fact that Mary Brennan was being kept in the barn was confirmed about half an hour later when Gerhart Schneider, his wife and another woman went into the barn and eventually came out with a young girl. Mick recognized her at once. She was set to work carrying buckets of water from a stream into first one house and then another. The fact that there was no sign of Evans or Buck seemed to confirm that they had left the girl and continued. There was, of course, the possibility that the two outlaws had been murdered by the community for some reason. He did not worry himself too much about this possibility.

There was no chance of Mick getting close enough to attract her attention and certainly not close enough to get her away. He reluctantly decided that the best time to attempt a rescue would be under the cover of darkness. At least darkness and the forest would provide some cover.

His first real chance came when, under the cover of the rapidly fading light, Mick and his companion moved from the safety of their hideout down towards the community. He hid behind a covered wagon which was close to the barn when Mary Brennan suddenly appeared carrying a slop bucket. He almost received the contents of it when he quietly hissed her name. It was obvious that she was confused and almost cried out, but he managed to stop her.

'Mary, it's me, Mick Nelson, Deputy Marshal, we were in that train together. I've come to take you back to your mother.'

'They bought me off those two men,' she choked. 'They want me to...'

'You can tell me later,' whispered Mick. 'Right now you just...' The woman he assumed to be Mrs Schneider suddenly appeared round the corner, her face lit up by an oil lamp she was carrying, and barked an order in German at Mary. Mary bobbed a slight curtsy and said that she was coming. Mrs Schneider disappeared from view although it was obvious that she was just round the corner. 'I'll wait here,' continued Mick. 'If you get the chance just walk out of there.' Mary said nothing and followed Mrs

Schneider. By that time the dog had disappeared although Mick sensed that he was close at hand.

Exactly how long he waited, Mick had no idea other than it seemed a very long time. Quite suddenly however, the shadowy figure of Mary Brennan ran from the house, heading straight towards where he was hiding. She was closely followed by one of the women and a young man who appeared to be carrying a rifle. Mick flattened himself on the ground hoping that neither Mary Brennan nor the other two would see him.

He was saved by the fact that Mary suddenly stumbled and fell. In an instant both the woman and the youth had grabbed her and hauled her back to the house. She was obviously being beaten for her attempted escape as he heard what he had to assume were her cries of pain.

It was obvious that for some time at least, she would be kept under much closer guard and would certainly not be allowed out of the house on her own again. This forced Mick to rethink his strategy

It was an oil lamp hanging outside the door which gave Mick the idea. His idea was certainly not one of which his superiors would have approved, but it seemed to him that he had no alternative other than to carry on to Lindsay and then return with a posse – if he could convince the authorities in Lindsay of his story. Even if he did reach Lindsay and return, he somehow knew that the girl would not be found. With this in mind he decided to act straight away.

He needed to create a diversion, a diversion during which he could take the girl and get her away and, since he had no guns, fire seemed a logical way to create such a diversion.

He waited some time for the activity in the house to subside, during which time several people came out and went to other houses. He was quite certain that Mary was not amongst them and the fact that she was still in the Schneider house appeared confirmed when he heard her cry out again, plainly being given another beating. Eventually, however, everything went very quiet and odd lights which had appeared in windows were extinguished. It seemed that the inhabitants of Wuppertal had retired for the night. Even the light outside the Schneider household had been extinguished, although the lamp itself was still hanging outside.

Once he was quite certain that everyone had retired for the night and reasonably sure that Mary Brennan was still in the Schneider house, he slowly and very quietly made his way to the door where he unhitched the lamp and shook it to ensure that there was still some oil in it. It did not sound or feel very full but there was certainly enough oil to at least start a fire.

He had already decided that his target was going to be the small barn where Mary had originally been kept, choosing as his actual target a small door at the rear of the building. This was the only building in which he could guarantee no member of the community was living and it also had the advantage of being full of dry hay and straw. He might have been certain that no human member of the community was in the barn, but he had not reckoned on some livestock being in it.

Some of that livestock made itself very noisily evident as he approached the barn. Even before he had unscrewed the cap on the oil lamp, several very large geese were suddenly rushing through a small opening at the side of the building and, necks stretched out down almost to the ground, were attacking him. He had heard about geese being better than guard dogs but this was the first time he had experienced anything like it first hand and he had to admit that they were very good, completely unafraid and that their beaks inflicted very painful injuries. However, he persisted, emptying the contents of the oil lamp on to a pile of hay alongside the door. He somehow managed to light the hay, despite the relentless attack of the geese and ran for cover under the wagon alongside the Schneider house, the geese in full and noisy pursuit.

By that time doors were starting to open as residents investigated the commotion but because the fire had been lit on the one side of the barn which was out of sight of anyone, it went unnoticed for some time, even though the flicker of flames was being reflected off nearby trees. Mick held his breath and waited, hoping that the fire would not be discovered before it had gained a good hold.

Strangely, although nearest to the barn, the occupants of the Schneider household were among the last to come out to investigate. Mick caught a brief glimpse of Mary Brennan, apparently dressed in a night shift, but as Gerhart Schneider and a youth, both carrying rifles, came out to investigate further, Mary was bundled back into the house. At least Mick now knew for certain that she was in the house and finding her would not be all that difficult.

The fire was suddenly discovered and had plainly taken a firm hold and while, at first, attempts were made to beat it out, it was obvious that they were fighting a losing battle. Eventually Gerhart Schneider called all able-bodied people, women and children, from the houses and a human chain was formed with buckets down to the river. However, it was noticeable that Mary Brennan was not amongst them. Mick took the opportunity to run into the Schneider house.

He was surprised to find Mary so easily, discovering her cowering in a corner of the main living-room. He did not speak to her, simply grabbed her arm and dragged her towards the door. It was true to say that she did not offer any resistance. However, he did not get the chance to take her outside. His way was suddenly barred by the youth who levelled the rifle at him.

Quite what happened or how he did it, Mick never did really work out, but suddenly he was kicking the youth to the floor, grabbing the rifle and ordering Mary to follow him. Once outside, the general confusion served as cover for their escape.

The fire was eventually brought under control, but not before the youth had recovered and had informed his father of what had happened. Schneider's first impulse was to go after Mick but his orders to one or two men brought a negative response and it was not until they were quite certain that the fire was well under control that he managed to gather some men together and explain what had happened. It was, somewhat reluctantly, agreed that four of them should follow Mick, kill him and retrieve the girl.

FIVE

Mick held Mary's hand tightly as they blundered through the forest, the rifle he had taken from the youth in his other hand. He had no idea how many bullets were in the rifle, but however many there were, at least now he did have something with which to fight if necessary.

At first he ignored Mary's complaints about being cold and tired, telling her that they had to get as far away from the community as possible. However, after what seemed at least an hour, it became increasingly obvious that he was driving her too hard and he was forced to relent and allow her to rest.

'We can't stay long,' he told her. 'I don't think they'll let us go so easily.'

'I can't go on,' she complained. 'I'm cold and tired. Surely they won't follow us in the dark? They won't be able to find us.'

'I wouldn't bank on it,' said Mick. 'Anyway, that's all the more reason for us to keep going, put as much distance between us and them as possible before daylight. Maybe when it does get light we'll be able to find somewhere to hide.' He felt something nuzzle his leg and knew that the dog had rejoined them. 'Well done, feller,' he said to the dog. 'Without you I might never have found her. Now, you just keep a look out for anyone an' let us know.'

'Those two men,' gasped Mary, shivering with cold, 'they sold me to them. That Mr Schneider said that he was going to marry me to his son.'

'I'd say you're a mite young to be married,' said Mick. 'I'm not surprised though, I have heard of things like that happening. I didn't see any young girls or women there.'

'One of the other women who spoke some English told me that they needed younger women,' said Mary. 'She said that she'd been taken in the same way except that it had been her parents who had sold her. She was very kind to me but didn't like anyone to know she'd been talking to me. What kind of parents would sell their own children?'

'It happens,' said Mick. 'It shouldn't but it does. I even heard that in the early days children were bought and sold in the same way they bought and sold slaves. Some of the early farmers bought children just to work their farms and I hear they treated them pretty bad. Now, are you ready to go again? We needn't run this time but we must keep going. If they find us the chances are that they'll kill me and take you back and if that happens it might be that nobody will ever find you.'

'I suppose so,' she moaned. 'I wish it wasn't so cold though.'

'Here, put my jacket on,' said Mick. 'It isn't much but it'll help.'

The direction their flight had taken them was something Mick could only guess at, although he was reasonably certain that they were heading the right way – towards Lindsay – but since it was totally dark it was equally possible that they were going round in circles.

It was about an hour later when Mick was suddenly aware that the dog was no longer with them, although by that time he was accustomed to it suddenly disappearing. However, it reappeared a few minutes later, this time quite agitated.

'I think we have company,' he whispered to Mary. 'It looks like there's some thick bushes over there. We'll hide and hope they don't find us.'

Once again the dog disappeared and

about five minutes after they had hidden in the bushes, lights could be seen amongst the trees from the direction they had come. Eventually it became clear that at least four men on horses were slowly approaching carrying flaming torches. They appeared to be examining the ground and Mick held his breath as they stopped and peered more closely at the ground close to where he and Mary had made their way into the bushes. It seemed that at least one member of the German community was a skilled tracker.

Mick flicked the safety catch off the rifle and took aim at the leading man just in case. He did not want to shoot unless he had to, knowing that it would only be a matter of time before they were overpowered if he did. Eventually the man who seemed to be in charge, who was also the expert tracker, was highlighted by one of the torches and proved to be Gerhart Schneider. After spending some time closely looking at the ground and talking between themselves, Schneider seemed to look in their direction although he eventually pointed ahead and they rode off, this time at a much faster pace, much to Mick's relief.

'I guess since we have to rest sometime, this is as good a place as any to wait until dawn,' he said. 'Try to get some sleep, we must move as soon as daylight comes. At least we now know they're ahead of us.'

'Can't we light a fire?' shivered Mary.

'And tell the whole world exactly where we are?' said Mick. 'I'm sorry, Mary. Here, you snuggle up to me, I'm cold too, maybe we can keep each other warm.'

She did as she was told, although she seemed a little self-conscious but within minutes she was asleep. It had been Mick's intention to remain awake and at first he had to fight to stop himself nodding off. He eventually gave up the struggle.

The morning was very cold, a hint of frost giving everything a certain crispness. Mary was shivering uncontrollably and complaining bitterly and for the first time Mick noticed that her shoes were in fact little more than thin slippers and that they were now almost worn through.

'It'll warm up,' he promised. 'I'm sorry I can't do somethin' about your shoes but I can't. We'll take it as easy as we can but it's goin' to be a long walk. Come on, we have to get to Lindsay so's I can get you back to your mother.'

'I'm used to not wearing shoes,' she said.

'I walk about without them all the time at home but I'm hungry and I don't feel very well. Will we reach this Lindsay place today?'

'I honestly don't know the answer to that,' he said, well aware that Lindsay was at least another two days. 'You'll feel better when it warms up.'

For the first time he had the opportunity to examine the rifle. It was a Nichols & Childs revolving cylinder rifle and, much to his relief, he discovered that its nine chambers were fully loaded. 'Maybe I'll be able to shoot a rabbit or a deer,' he said. 'I'll see. First though, we have to find out where Schneider and his friends are.'

The dog had returned sometime during the night and now Mick pointed ahead, telling it to let them know if anyone was nearby. It appeared to understand what was needed and raced off.

Following the tracks left by the four horsemen was very easy even to an untrained eye such as Mick's; the ground was quite soft and their hoof prints were very plain. He decided that since the Germans knew the forest they would know the route to Lindsay and that he would follow them. However, after a time it became clear that they, the Germans, had not stopped to look for signs of their quarry's progress and this made Mick uneasy. It seemed obvious to him that they must have realized that they were ahead of him and the girl and that they had ridden on with some definite objective in mind. In this respect the Germans had a distinct advantage. They knew the territory and Mick did not. All he could do was keep going and hope for the best.

It was also very obvious that Mary's condition was deteriorating rapidly. She was demanding more frequent rests and her breathing was becoming very laboured. By midday she coughed up some blood and simply lay down and closed her eyes, even refusing some water. She was plainly completely worn out and very ill.

It was all Mick could do to keep her awake. He had heard somewhere that it was vital to keep anyone in her condition awake. He tried coaxing her to carry on and although she did respond briefly, they had not travelled more than fifty yards before she suddenly collapsed, this time completely unconscious. All his attempts to revive her proved fruitless. The dog also seemed very worried and tried licking her face and gently pawing at her arm.

There was no real shelter where she had fallen and Mick picked her up in his arms, surprised at how light she was. After about ten minutes he came across a small, sandstone cliff, little more than a ridge, which provided some protection and, after listening to her rasping chest and feeling her profusely sweating forehead, he knew that it was impossible to take her any further.

Ignoring the danger to himself and in an attempt to give her some warmth he lit a fire and then pondered his next move. He was well aware that it was now only a matter of when and not if he was found by the Germans.

About half an hour later a low growl from the dog told him that the Germans were close by and he automatically took his rifle and hid behind a nearby tree stump. The dog had disappeared. About five minutes later he was aware of someone moving amongst the trees and, giving a quick glance at Mary, he came to a decision.

'Schneider!' he called. 'I know you're out there.'

'I would have been surprised if you had not known,' came the response. 'I think you saw us last night. We knew you had hidden in the bushes but we also knew that you are armed. We are in no great hurry. You should never have taken the girl. We have come to take her back. It is a pity, a pity for you that is, we cannot allow you to live. It is nothing personal you understand, simply a matter of our survival.'

'She's in a bad way,' called Mick. 'I think she's caught pneumonia. She'll die if she doesn't get some treatment pretty damned quick and the only place I know where she might get seen to is back at your place. I won't stop you taking her back, but you can be pretty damned certain that once I get to Lindsay I'll be back with a posse.'

'You will never reach Lindsay,' replied Schneider. 'Unfortunately for you, you have interfered in something which need not have concerned you.'

'In a way it was my fault she came to be out here,' replied Mick. 'I guess that makes me responsible for her. It's you that's at fault, you shouldn't go round buyin' girls off outlaws.'

'We did not know for certain that they were outlaws,' said Schneider. 'What we did is not unknown elsewhere and as far as I am aware is not illegal. We are in need of young women.'

'Then I suggest you go to somewhere like Lindsay,' called Mick.

'That is something we have tried,' said Schneider. 'Unfortunately it seems that most people do not like our way of life. This means that we have to resort to other methods to ensure our survival.'

'Even if that means killin' me,' responded Mick. 'Are you goin' to murder everyone who happens to pass through if they have a young girl or woman with them? It has to stop somewhere, Schneider, so it might as well stop here before it gets any worse, or do you always do things like this? I'm walkin' out of here, Schneider. If you have any concern at all for the girl you'll take her back with you and take care of her simply because she's ill. Just remember this though, there are folk who know where I went and why and if you kill me you'll be killing a deputy marshal. The authorities don't take kindly to the murder of any lawman. They'll organize a marshal's posse and if they do that there's no escape.

'They will never find your body,' said Schneider. 'There is a lot of forest and wilderness out here. Now, the next move is up to you, Marshal. You can attempt your escape and leave the girl to us but you can be quite certain that we shall hunt you down should you manage to elude us, which I doubt you can. Even now you have no escape route. I know that you are armed with the rifle you took from my son and that it is fully loaded and I have no doubt that you are a very good shot. So, for the moment, it would seem that we have something of a stand-off. However, as you say, she is very ill and the longer you hold us off the worse she will become. If she dies it is you who will be responsible for her death, not us.'

Mick was aware that two of them had taken up position about thirty yards either side of where he was, close to the cliff, leaving Schneider and the other man in front of him. This effectively meant that, with the cliff behind him, he was surrounded. He looked about for other possible escape routes and it was plain that there was none that he could even contemplate. Suddenly his eyes latched on to a tall tree about three or four yards to his left which appeared to reach the top of the cliff and looked relatively easy to climb.

He did not give the matter a second thought as he snatched his jacket and, clutching the rifle, raced to the tree and started to climb it. Several bullets shattered the bark close to his face and body and he felt one graze his leg, but he continued climbing.

Further bullets followed his ascent but somehow he managed to reach a strong branch which was level with the cliff top and, taking a chance on being shot, walked out along it, holding on to a higher branch. He felt another bullet hit his leg but gave it little thought as he launched himself across the three foot gap to the cliff top.

His leg hurt and he was aware of blood flowing down into his boot but he had no choice but to keep on running. He followed the cliff top for about sixty or seventy yards before the ground below suddenly rose up to meet it. He had seen two riders below following his progress but, luckily for him, even before where the cliff top and the lower ground met, it was so thickly wooded and strewn with fallen branches and trees that it was virtually impossible for a horse to get through.

After about ten minutes negotiating fallen trees and moss covered rocks he breathed a sigh of relief and allowed himself a short rest and time to examine his wounds. The one was little more than a scratch but the second bullet had entered his calf and appeared to be lodged. He tied his kerchief round the wound in an attempt to stem the bleeding and then continued through the thick bush. A rustle in the undergrowth close by made him swing round, rifle at the ready but once again he sighed with relief and lowered the gun.

'You should've barked or somethin',' he said. 'I might've shot you.' The dog responded by wagging its tail. 'OK, feller, what do we do now?' he continued. 'I'm glad you're here though, you can hear an' smell things I can't. Keep your cars open for those Germans. They know where they're goin' which is more than you an' I do.'

Still reasonably certain that he was heading in the right direction, Mick quite deliberately followed the denser sections of the forest in an attempt to discourage them from following, even though it made his own progress that much slower. There were times when he was forced to cross ground that was rather more open although he had now come to rely very much on the dog and on all but one of these occasions the animal did not give any indication that anything was wrong.

The one time that it did react he came

face to face with a solitary wolf, which seemed almost as surprised as he was. They eyed each other warily for a few moments before it suddenly turned and was soon lost in the undergrowth. In fact Mick had almost come to the conclusion that he was not being followed and his confidence was such that he even shot a small deer.

By early evening, he had found shelter under an overhanging rock alongside a small but clear stream. Wisely or unwisely, his confidence was now such that he lit a fire, gutted and skinned the deer and skewered cuts of it over the flames. During his escape up the tree, he had been forced to leave his cooking utensils behind. The meat was very welcome both to him and the dog and, as the darkness drew in, they both settled down for a well earned sleep.

'I heard it too,' Mick whispered in response to the dog's whimper and scraping at his arm. 'Which way are they? Go find 'em feller.' The dog needed no further instruction and disappeared into the darkness. Mick had to assume that it had headed off in the direction of whoever or whatever had woken them both.

As a precaution, Mick hid behind a moss

covered rock, rifle at the ready, listening intently. Had he been alone he might well have assumed that the sound he had heard was either his imagination or made by some animal. The dog's reaction however, convinced him that it was not his imagination and that it was not some forest animal.

It was at least another ten minutes before he heard the crack of a fallen branch being broken under foot, followed by another period of silence. He did wonder just what the dog was doing all this time since he had neither heard nor seen anything of him. His wait was finally brought to an end as he saw a large, dark figure very slowly approaching the dying embers of the fire.

'Hold it right where you are,' Mick ordered, raising the rifle. 'I've got you covered.'

'Seems like you got a good dog on your side too,' came the response. 'Hold your fire, mister.'

'I was expectin' the Germans,' replied Mick. 'You don't sound like no German to me.'

'Germans!' grunted the man, 'Oh yeh, you mean them funny folk from back at the settlement. Now why in the hell should you be expectin' them?'

'It's a long story,' said Mick. 'OK, you can come in, but don't try makin' no sudden moves.'

The figure moved closer to what was left of the fire, grunted something and threw some more wood on the embers. Mick too moved closer, his rifle at the ready and, after a large, bearded face had eyed him closely for a few moments, he lowered it, reasonably certain that the man presented no danger. Even the dog, which had followed the man, seemed to know that there was no threat.

'Luke Short,' said the man. 'I see by your badge that you're a sheriff or somethin'.'

'Deputy Marshal Mick Nelson,' responded Mick.

'Now what in the hell brings a deputy marshal an' a dog way out here?' grinned Luke. 'Me, I'm a hunter, furs is my game an' I live out here. My cabin is about a day to the east. I might as well not bother with it though, I'm hardly ever there.'

'I might ask what brings a fur-trapper out here at this time of night as well?' said Mick. 'I don't have any idea what time it is except that it isn't dawn yet. So what brings you snoopin' round at this time of night?'

'I guess you could say that I'm just nosy,'

said Luke. 'I saw your fire. If you know what you're lookin' at out here, things like fires stand out a mile, even in the forest. So what's this between you an' the Germans? I've been through their settlement a few times an' they allus struck me as bein' a peaceable lot, strange but peaceable.'

'It'll take too long to explain,' said Mick. 'It's beginnin' to look like I've given them the slip though. Either that or they've decided not to follow me for some reason.'

'Don't know what they was followin' you for an' I ain't particularly int'rested,' said Luke. 'I ain't seen no sign of 'em an' I don't miss much.'

'I can believe that,' said Mick.

'That meat smells good,' said Luke, picking up a piece of cooked meat. He did not wait for permission as his teeth tore into it. 'I ain't eaten since the day afore yesterday,' he continued through a full mouth. 'Been too busy settin' traps. So, the Germans are after you, you sure must've upset 'em; like I say, they're normally a peaceable lot. Still, it ain't none of my business.'

'How far is it to Lindsay?' asked Mick.

Luke thought for a moment, tore some more meat off the bone he was holding and once again spoke through a full mouth. 'I reckon you should make it by tomorrow night providin' you don't get no hold-ups. Maybe just about sunset. It all depends.'

'Depends on what?' asked Mick.

'On how fast you can walk,' grinned Luke. 'Mind if I stay here for the rest of the night? It's probably about four hours till sun-up.'

'Be my guest,' said Mick, in a way quite pleased to have some company. 'Maybe you can answer a question. I found another trapper way back before the German community. He'd been murdered an' I know who by. Big man he was, much the same build as you. His cabin wasn't too far from the railroad. I can't be sure why he was murdered other than for his guns.'

'Only feller I know out that way is Ben Wiesnesky,' replied Luke. 'Ain't seen him for more'n twelve months though. We don't normally work another feller's territory. Murdered you say? Somehow I don't need no second guess who did it. There was a couple of mean lookin' fellers out this way maybe a week ago now. They warn't regular bush men, more like your regular gun-fighters I'd say.'

'Saul Evans an' Harold Buck,' said Mick. 'You're right, they are gunfighters, wanted outlaws. I was escortin' 'em back when the train was derailed an' they escaped. They took a young girl as hostage an' I went after them.'

Luke nodded knowingly and laughed. 'A young girl you say?' he said. 'Now I guess that explains just why them Germans is after you. I heard tell that they was desperate for young women. I even heard tell they ain't above payin' travellers for their daughters. I'd say they bought the girl off your two outlaws but that you found her an' tried to get her away.'

'Got it first time,' said Mick. 'I did get her away too. Only problem was that she got sick, too sick to carry on. I reckon they've taken her back.'

'An' they daren't let you get to Lindsay,' said Luke. 'Now me an' them Germans know this territory an' it's my guess they is holed up right now at Navaho Pass knowin' that you'd have to go through there.'

'And how far is this Navaho Pass?' asked Mick.

'Three, maybe four hours' walkin',' said Luke. 'Believe me, once you're there, there ain't no other way you can go. They'll be able to pick you off any time they've a mind to.'

'OK,' said Mick, 'so I don't go through this pass.'

'Now that's easier said than done,' said Luke. 'There is a way but unless you know it you'd never find it.'

'So tell me about it,' invited Mick.

Luke laughed once again. 'That's easier said than done as well,' he said. 'This trail ends up in a big basin, sheer cliffs all round. To get round it you have to strike off in a different direction from here on. Once you reach the basin, particularly since you're on foot, you can be seen from miles away an', since I assume they have horses, they'd soon catch you.'

'OK,' said Mick, 'So point me in the right direction from here. I'll find my way even if it takes another week.'

Luke sat thoughtfully for a few moments, absently prodding the fire. 'Son,' he said eventually, 'I'm a law abidin' man. Personally I don't give a damn what happens to the girl, she could do worse than live with the Germans. The thing is, Ben Wiesnesky was a friend of mine an' I don't like it when my friends get murdered. You make me a promise that you'll find his killers an' I'll even lead you most of the way.'

'I was goin' after them anyway,' said Mick.

'I have my pride too. I ain't never lost a prisoner before an' I don't want to start a habit. You're on.'

'OK,' agreed Luke. 'Now, get yourself some sleep, it's goin' to be a long, hard walk an' it'll mean you gettin' to Lindsay a day later.'

'What's another day?' said Mick.

SIX

Mick, Luke and the dog were on their way as soon as the first hint of dawn highlighted the mountains to the east. It had been a cold night with quite a heavy frost which was all the more noticeable as they crossed the edge of a flat, open plain, about three miles wide. There was even ice at the edge of the many rivulets which criss-crossed the plain.

Luke kept to the extreme edge of the plain, close to the forest, stopping once to point out where the Germans were most likely to be hiding on the far side, although there was no obvious sign that they were there. He also pointed directly ahead at a seemingly impenetrable wall of rock rising to about 3,000 or 4,000 feet and now about two or three miles in front of them. He almost casually told Mick that they had some climbing to do, an observation which appeared very obvious. As far as Mick was concerned though, from that distance, there did not appear to be any way to either climb or find a way through, but he had to give way to the trapper's evident greater knowledge and experience.

When they did eventually reach the base of the wall of rock, there was even less evidence of any way of getting through. Climbing appeared completely out of the question. The sheer rock had a glasslike sheen to it and footholds were non-existent. However, Luke unerringly led the way between some large boulders and into a very narrow fissure barely wide enough to accommodate their bodies. At one point they were forced to crawl on their hands and knees for about thirty yards through what was little more than a narrow tunnel.

Once they were through the tunnel they had to climb an almost vertical pile of loose rocks for another sixty or seventy feet. The dog seemed to be enjoying himself as he bounded from rock to rock. Luke did make the very obvious observation that it was lucky they did not have horses and that they were fortunate it was not the rainy season since the way they had come would then have been an impassable torrent of water.

Once at the top of the rocks there was another narrow fissure, although this time it widened out the further into it they went. By mid-afternoon and after a lot of climbing, they were standing atop a sheer, 4,000-foot-high cliff with the plain they had left some eight hours earlier directly below them. Mick was quite disheartened to think that they had spent the best part of the day climbing and had not made any obvious headway.

Although they had taken brief rests during the day, they had never stopped for long but on this occasion Luke took the opportunity to take a good rest and at first Mick did not object.

'They're down there,' said Luke, pointing down at a narrow pass situated at the end of the plain. 'You can just make out some horses.' He pointed insistently and eventually Mick was able to make out what did appear to be horses. However, without Luke to point them out he would never have been able to see them.

Interest in the scene far below quickly palled as Mick was becoming rather more concerned about the condition of his leg. The wound had become very red and his leg had swollen quite a lot and was becoming increasingly painful. Luke examined the injury and made the obvious diagnosis that it was turning bad ways and that he needed the services of a doctor. Mick made some scathing remark about the trapper's ability to state the obvious as though he was making some profound observation. Luke seemed to take this as a compliment.

'How far is to Lindsay?' asked Mick.

'Another day at least,' said Luke. 'We've made better time than I expected so far. Still, that's the worst over an' done with. From here on it's mostly downhill an' definitely easier goin'.'

'Then let's go,' urged Mick, anxious to reach Lindsay and have his leg attended to. 'I don't fancy bein' stuck out here with a leg full of gangrene.'

'I reckon you should make it in time,' said Luke. 'I've seen worse'n that an' they didn't lose their legs. Mind, if you don't get it seen to pretty damned quick you'll end up losin' it for sure.'

'I'd rather not take that chance,' said Mick. 'Just point me in the right direction an' I'll find my own way.'

'OK, son,' sighed Luke. 'I reckon since I've come this far I might as well take you all the way. I ain't been in Lindsay for more'n six months an' I guess I could do with some supplies. Just give me another five minutes. My bones are a whole lot older'n yours an' my joints don't work too well sometimes.

They tell me it's old age, but I ain't that old. Leastways I don't think so.'

'How old are you?' asked Mick, not really interested.

'I tried workin' it out once,' said Luke. 'I ain't too clever when it comes to book learnin' an' such, but I worked it out at somethin' over a hundred, but that don't seem right to me.'

'I'd say you did work it out wrong,' said Mick. 'I ain't never heard of nobody over a hundred years old, 'ceptin' that feller in the bible. Methuselah I think he was called. I'd say you was sixty at the most.'

'That ain't too old,' said Luke. 'OK, I'll settle for sixty.'

'Didn't your ma ever tell you when you were born?' asked Mick.

'Don't remember her very well,' replied Luke. 'I was told she died givin' birth to another child, a boy they told me, so I guess I have me a brother somewhere. Anyhow, I was given to some farmers but they treated me so damned bad I up an' left the first chance I had. I guess I must've been twelve or thirteen when I left. I never did know who my pa was an' I was told my ma wasn't too sure. I took to the hills an' I've been here ever since. I lost all track of time an' in any

115

case time don't mean a thing up here, 'cept knowin' when it's spring, summer or winter an' that don't take much workin' out. Sure, I'll settle for bein' sixty.'

Five minutes proved to be closer to fifteen minutes but eventually they were on their way again, although this time Mick was rather more conscious of his leg which was becoming more painful, although he was inclined to put this down to his mind rather than actual fact.

Luke's claim that it was mainly downhill from that point onwards hardly seemed to bear close examination as far as Mick was concerned; he was quite convinced that they had climbed even higher. However, the truth of the claim was proved when, on looking back after about an hour, it was obvious that they had been descending and apparently by quite a lot as he recognized a landmark they had passed level with as now being at least 500 feet above them.

By early evening they had descended until they were only a few hundred feet above another wide, flat plain, at the far side of which, according to Luke, was the town of Lindsay. His estimation was that they would reach the town by mid-afternoon the following day at the latest.

Mick was surprised when Luke elected to rest up for the night in the mountains. His unasked query was answered when Luke explained that it was purely a precaution against the Germans checking that they had somehow avoided the pass.

'They won't come up here,' said Luke, 'an' even if they did we could defend ourselves. Personally I don't reckon they will check, but it's better safe than sorry. As far as I know there's only about three people who know the way we've just come an' none of 'em ain't the Germans. They'd never have any cause to find out.' Mick was forced to agree to this logic.

The actual time of their arrival in Lindsay was midday. It had been Mick who had pushed the pace despite, or perhaps even because of, the ever increasing pain in his leg which, he had eventually decided, was not in his imagination. The first thing Mick did was to report to the sheriff's office, briefly explain who he was and why he was there and ask to be guided to the doctor. He left the dog with Luke and it appeared to know what was required of it.

'I've seen worse,' grunted a young man who was about the same age as Mick and who hardly seemed old enough to be a qualified doctor. Mick had doubts as to whether or not the doctor had seen worse. 'There's a bullet still in there, lodged up against the bone,' continued the young man. 'I'll have to take it out.'

'Have you ever done anythin' like this before?' asked Mick. 'You seem a mite young to be a doctor.'

The young man smiled knowingly. 'And you seem a mite young to be a marshal,' he countered. 'I have certificates to prove I'm qualified. Do you have any certificates to prove that you are qualified as a marshal? I don't suppose you have, you don't need certificates for that kind of thing.'

'I'm only a deputy marshal,' said Mick. 'OK, Doc, I take your point. I guess we all have to start somewhere. It's just that almost every doctor I've ever met has been in his forties or older.'

'And probably not qualified,' said the young man, grinning broadly. 'I know two or three men like that, all claiming to be qualified doctors but the only real quali-fication they have is years of experience. One of them was actually a veterinarian before he turned to doctoring people and another was nothing more than a barber. He claimed he was qualified because surgeons and barbers used to be the same thing. The choice is yours, Marshal, let me take that bullet out and clean up your leg or you'll end up having it amputated at least and you'll probably even die. It's a free country – so they tell me – and I suppose everyone is entitled to go to hell in their own way.'

'Now?' queried Mick, apprehensively.

'Sure, why not?' said the doctor. 'I've got the time.'

'I ain't got no money,' said Mick. 'I had it stolen way up in the mountains.'

'I'd say your credit's good,' said the doctor, laughing. 'Come on, let's get you on the table.'

Less than half an hour later, Mick hobbled from the doctor's office, uncertain as to whether or not his leg was more painful or less painful than before. He had to admit that the young doctor certainly seemed to know what he was doing. Although the operation had been painful enough, it had not been quite as bad as Mick had expected. In fact, upon reflection, most of the pain had been in anticipation of the sharp scalpel than the actual use of it.

He had known men be offered large

amounts of whiskey before undergoing such operations, but this young doctor had simply laughed at the suggestion. His leg was now fully bandaged and he had been instructed to attend the office the following afternoon to have the wound re-dressed. Mick expressed doubts as to whether or not he would be able to attend, explaining to the doctor about the girl. He was advised to keep the wound clean at least until it had healed over.

He found Luke and the dog in the seediest of the four saloons in Lindsay and had to ask the trapper for the price of a large whiskey, something he felt he needed, although he was not normally much of a whiskey man. Unlike the whiskey he had sampled in Greenhills, this was obviously the real thing and not home-made moonshine.

'I'll have to get me some cash,' he said to Luke. 'I'll talk to the sheriff, maybe he can get me some and charge it to the governor's office. I'll have to get him to organize a posse as well. I have to go back to that settlement and get that girl back.'

'I reckon you'd be wastin' your time,' said Luke. 'You probably didn't see him an' probably wouldn't've recognized him anyway, but when we came into town one of them Germans rode out like the devil himself was after him. It won't be long before they all know you're here an' when they do that girl will be spirited away. They might even kill her.'

'Damn!' oathed Mick. 'That makes it all the more essential that I get a posse together as quickly as possible. I'm going to talk to the sheriff right now.'

'An' the best of luck,' said Luke. 'One thing I do know about folk in Lindsay is that there ain't nothin' can make 'em move fast if'n they don't want to. I'll be down at the roomin' house behind the livery if you want me or the dog.'

Mick made his way back to the sheriff's office where Sheriff Dan Saunders listened to his story but showed little sign of concern or real interest. He made some observation about the German community being outside his jurisdiction, pointing out that he, Deputy Marshal Mick Nelson, had more authority than a mere sheriff did to organize a posse under the circumstances. He also pointed out that a posse was normally made up of volunteers and that it was most unlikely that he would be able to raise any such volunteers in Lindsay.

'Don't you care what happens to the girl?' demanded Mick. 'Hell, man, she's only twelve years old.'

'Some twelve-year-olds are married an' even have children,' replied the sheriff. 'That happens a lot, 'specially up in the mountains. Things out here ain't the same as back in the big cities. Kids out here grow up a whole lot quicker.'

'So you're not going to do anythin'?' rasped Mick. 'I guess kidnappin' is somethin' that happens every day as well.'

'I've been sheriff here for the past ten years an' I ain't never come across a case of kidnappin' before,' admitted Saunders. 'Like I said, them Germans are out of my territory, and so as far as I'm concerned they ain't done nothin' wrong. You're a federal deputy marshal, you have all the necessary authority, it's up to you to do what you think best.'

'Then as a federal deputy marshal,' said Mick, 'I demand co-operation.'

'You can make all the demands you've a mind to,' replied the sheriff, completely unruffled. 'I was appointed by the town council to look after law an' order in Lindsay County an' Lindsay County ends where the mountains start. I ain't that hard-hearted though. Tell you what I'll do. I'll talk to the council an' let them decide. If they agree, I'll get you a posse together.'

'How long will that take?' sighed Mick, realizing that it was about the best he was going to get for the moment.

'Give me a couple of hours,' said the sheriff.

'OK,' Mick reluctantly agreed. 'The next question is, did you have two strangers through here in the past week?'

'The two escaped outlaws?' said the sheriff. 'Sure, I reckon we had them through here. I didn't know then they was outlaws though. They stayed two days – or was it three? – I ain't sure. Anyhow, they behaved themselves while they was here an' I never had no cause to suspect who they were. I do check Wanted posters when we get strangers through but I sure didn't have no flyer on them. That ain't all that unusual though. Sometimes we get flyers on men who've already been arrested.'

'When they left, which way did they go?' asked Mick.

'Due south,' replied Saunders. 'I know that on account of I was comin' back from the Graham Ranch when I passed 'em. I was out there dealin' with a half-breed who'd run amok with a knife.'

'And the German community is due north,' sighed Mick. 'OK, as far as I'm concerned the girl comes first. You go and explain to your council what happened. If they want to talk to me you'll find me around somewhere. Luke Short, the trapper, will probably know where I am.'

'Yeh, I seen you ride in with old Luke,' said the sheriff. 'It ain't often he comes into town. One of these years he'll just stop comin' altogether an' maybe one day someone'll find his bones up there in the hills, picked clean by buzzards an' coyotes an' they'll maybe wonder who he was an' how he died. Most likely though they'll just ignore the bones.'

Much to his surprise, the decision of the town council was that they should provide Deputy Marshal Mick Nelson with all the assistance he required, including sending a telegram to the state capital to seek authorization to supply Mick with everything he needed in the form of a horse, guns and money. For some reason it was a decision which apparently did not go down too well with Sheriff Dan Saunders, but he grudgingly accepted it. However, by the time cooperation had been agreed, the sun had dropped below the western horizon and the task of finding volunteers to form a posse was deferred until the following morning.

Again, surprisingly since Saunders had been quite certain that there would be none, ten volunteers were found and Mick was supplied with a horse and guns. The volunteers were also supplied with rifles from the sheriff's armoury. However, just as the ritual of swearing in had been completed, five horsemen rode into town.

'Looks like we don't have to go after 'em,' observed Saunders. 'That's Gerhart Schneider an' if I ain't mistaken that girl you're after is right there with 'em.' The group of Germans pulled up outside the sheriff's office, Schneider sneering slightly at Mick.

'We meet again, Marshal,' he said, smiling thinly. 'As you can see, the girl, Mary, is much improved. In fact she is so much better that we decided to bring her back to you. We had to come in to town for some supplies sometime so we decided to combine the two things. You did the right thing in leaving her with us, she would probably have died had she not received treatment when she did.'

This sudden and unexpected turn of events threw Mick completely although it was obvious to him at least as to why it had happened this way.

'I wonder if you would have bothered if it hadn't been for one of you seein' me arrive in town,' he said. 'I somehow don't think so. Maybe I'll still have you arrested for kidnappin'.'

'Kidnapping, Marshal!' said Schneider raising his eyebrows. 'Quite the contrary. We took her from those two outlaws because we were very concerned about her safety with such men.'

'Then why didn't you hand her over to me when I came through,' challenged Mick.

'Marshal!' said Schneider, smiling broadly. 'Other than that badge you are wearing, we had no proof that you were who you claimed to be. We had to be certain that we were not simply handing Mary over to another undesirable type. By the time we had decided that you were who you claimed to be, you had made a very melodramatic and totally unnecessary bid to rescue her. We followed you to offer our assistance but by the time we found you she had developed pneumonia.'

'If you were tryin' to help,' said Mick, 'how

do you explain the bullet in my leg? How do you explain me havin' to climb a tree to save my life?'

'I can offer no explanation as to why you found it necessary to climb that tree, Marshal,' said Schneider. 'The bullet is more easily explained by the fact that one of us thought that you were about to shoot at him. It is only natural that a man should protect himself. I can assure you that had any of us wished to kill you, you would not be talking to us now.'

'All very slick!' hissed Mick, turning to Sheriff Saunders. 'You can't believe a word of that, can you?'

'Why not?' shrugged the sheriff. 'It all sounds perfectly likely as far as I'm concerned, an' they have brought the girl back. That don't seem like the actions of kidnappers to me.'

'The only reason they brought her back is because I managed to avoid them,' insisted Mick. 'They knew that if they didn't hand her over I'd be out there with a posse.'

'That was indeed one of our prime considerations,' agreed Schneider. He looked at Sheriff Saunders. 'It was obvious to us that the marshal was in some way mentally unbalanced at the time and since we are a peaceful community we did not want to risk him riding in and shooting the place up and possibly killing or injuring some of our people. To prevent such a thing happening we decided to bring the girl to Lindsay.'

'That sure sounds perfectly reasonable as far I'm concerned,' said Saunders. 'OK, Marshal, you've got your girl back. I guess I can disband this posse.' He nodded at the men, most of whom appeared quite relieved. 'What you goin' to do with her now though? You can't take her with you if you intend goin' after them outlaws.'

'Where's the nearest railroad station?' asked Mick. 'I'll get her on to a train first an' then go after Buck and Evans.'

'That'll be Coloma,' replied the sheriff. 'That's about a day an' a half south-west.'

'I remember goin' through there when I took the railroad out to Greenhills,' nodded Mick. 'That'll do fine.'

'It ain't too far out of your way either,' observed Saunders. 'It could even be that your outlaws went through there, although the way they was goin' I'd say Gartree was the most likely place.'

Mick was tempted to start out there and then, but a glance at Mary told him that perhaps she was not quite as fit as Schneider claimed and he somewhat reluctantly decided to postpone what would be a tiring journey for her, at least until Doc Jameson had examined her.

During the day authorization to supply Mick with whatever he needed came through and Mick also sent another telegram to say that Mary Brennan was safe and would be placed on a train in Coloma.

The transfer of a horse, saddle, guns and ammunition was made with little fuss. All that was required was his signature on a receipt. However, in the true bureaucratic traditions of all banks, the task of supplying Mick with $200 was anything but simple.

The president of the bank insisted on everything being signed in triplicate with counter-signatures by both Sheriff Saunders and the mayor of Lindsay. At one point it seemed that the money would not be forthcoming without further proof of identity from Mick. Eventually, however, the money was counted out in front of the necessary witnesses and handed to Mick as though millions were passing hands instead of $200.

Doc Jameson pronounced Mary fit but in a weakened condition and supplied her with some medicine, although he did advise against her travelling for a few days. Mick, however, was not prepared to lose any more time and Mary insisted that she was now well enough to travel and that she really wanted to get home.

In all this Mick had completely forgotten about Luke Short and the dog. Eventually he found them both in the same saloon as before, although this time Mick bought the whiskey.

Mick patted the dog and shook his head a little sadly. 'I guess this really is the end of the road for us,' he said, choking slightly. 'I'm goin' to have to do some pretty hard ridin'.' The dog licked his hand and nuzzled its head against his leg. 'You saved my life a couple of times an' if it hadn't been for you I'd never've found the girl. I wish I could take you with me but I don't think you'd be too happy.'

'I was wonderin' what you was goin' to do with him,' said Luke. 'I had me a dog once, not too long ago but he upped an' died on me. He was pretty old too, well over sixty in dog years I guess.'

'Then there ain't no problem,' said Mick. 'You take him, he'd be far happier runnin' the hills an' forest with you than tied up in some backyard with me.'

'Sure, I'll take him,' grunted Luke, stroking the dog. 'I guess that decision's up to him though.'

'OK, feller,' nodded Mick. 'You know the score, I can't take you, leastways I won't be able to look after you properly. Now with Luke here, you'll have all the freedom you want.' Mick stood up and walked slowly towards the door. The dog seemed a little uncertain at first but after looking at Mick and then Luke, he returned to sit under the table at Luke's feet. 'I guess that's it then,' said Mick, trying to quell a lump in his throat. 'Cheerio, feller.' He turned and left the saloon feeling both pleased and sad. He never did see Luke Short or the dog again.

SEVEN

Mick had Mary Brennan checked out by the young doctor who pronounced her fit enough to travel provided she was not pushed too hard. Mick also tried to borrow a wagon and horse but, not surprisingly as far as he was concerned, nobody seemed all that interested in helping. Most claimed, not unreasonably, that it was not often that anyone had the need to go into Coloma, which they would have to do to retrieve the wagon. In the end he was forced to allow her to ride up behind him since buying another horse would be a waste of money.

They eventually set out just after dawn the following morning and he had been assured that the road to Coloma was good and flat all the way and that he should reach the town by noon the following day at the latest. Although experience had taught him not to put too much credence on such assurances, for once, it appeared that he had not been misinformed.

They set up camp for the night beside a

small river where Mary showed herself to be a good cook and soon prepared a tasty meal using various ingredients Mick had bought in Lindsay. He was very pleased that she elected to cook for him since he did not count himself amongst the better cooks of the world and it did give her something to do.

He took the opportunity to question her more closely about her treatment in the German community and her answers largely confirmed what he suspected. Whilst she had been ill they had apparently treated her very well and he had to concede that but for that she may well have died. She had also heard the heated conversation that had taken place when one of their community returned from Lindsay. She had, of course, not understood a word of what they were saying but the younger woman who had befriended her had translated.

It seemed that the community was more or less equally divided on what to do and it had only been Gerhart Schneider's insistence which had assured her freedom. Schneider had not been prepared to risk the wrath of the law and the inevitable disruption to their way of life. However, despite her story confirming what he already knew,

Mick was well aware that he would never be able to prove anything, so he reluctantly decided to forget the matter.

Coloma was reached, as predicted, shortly after midday the following day and once again Mick reported to the sheriff's office, this time receiving a better reception than he had in Lindsay.

'They got through to the wrecked train three days after the accident,' said Sheriff Turner. 'They said somethin' about you goin' off after them outlaws an' the girl. To be honest nobody ever expected to see you or her alive again.'

'Glad to be able to prove everyone wrong,' said Mick. 'All I have to do now is get her on the next train an' back to her mother.'

'Now there is another problem,' said the sheriff. 'We ain't had a train through here since the accident, although I hear tell that they've repaired the line an' cleared the wreckage. The station master did say somethin' about a train comin' through tomorrow though, but whether or not it does remains to be seen. I guess the first we'll know about it will be when it arrives in town.'

'I was kinda hopin' to get her aboard before that,' said Mick. 'Evans an' Buck have had a good start on me.

'They might even be on the other side of the country by now,' nodded Turner. 'Personally I'd give up the idea of goin' after them. Men like that don't suddenly change their ways. They'll eventually end up bein' caught or maybe killed.'

'Only problem with that is how many folk will they kill in the meantime,' said Mick. 'They was my responsibility so I feel beholden to get them back. It seems likely that they headed for some place called Gartree.'

'Silver an' lead minin' town,' said Turner. 'About a three day ride from here. Easy goin' though, even if the trail does go through the mountains. I can't see them hangin' about there too long. Those miners can be a real mean bunch if anyone crosses 'em. Anyhow, there ain't nothin' in Gartree would make any man stop longer'n he had to.'

'In the meantime I have to hang about waitin' for a train which might or might not come,' muttered Mick. 'I'll send a wire ahead sayin' that she'll be on the next train.'

Sheriff Turner seemed to be thinking and after a few moments looked up at Mick and smiled. 'Tell you what,' he said. 'Me an'

Grace – she's my wife – we'll take her in until the train comes through an' then make sure she's safely aboard.'

'Won't your wife mind?' asked Mick.

'Naw, shouldn't think so,' said Turner. 'She'll understand.' He looked at Mary who had been sitting silently. 'You won't mind stayin' with us for a while, will you?'

'I don't want to be any trouble,' Mary replied quietly. 'I think I'd like that though and Mr Nelson does have more important things to do than play nursemaid to someone like me.'

'That's settled then,' the sheriff decided. 'I'll take you round to meet Grace – I mean Mrs Turner. Now, Marshal, what's your next move?'

'Get my leg seen to, it still hurts,' said Mick. He went on to give a brief explanation of what had happened between him and the Germans. Mary's ordeal with the German community was also told to Mrs Turner who seemed horrified that anyone should even consider a twelve-year-old as being of an age to marry.

The telegraph message informing of the arrangements for Mary was sent and Mick went to see the doctor, an older man who looked more like a doctor ought to look as far as Mick was concerned. The older man sniffed slightly at the mention of Doc Jameson of Lindsay but had the good manners to concede that he had performed a satisfactory operation and that the pain was due to nothing more than Mick not resting his leg enough. He had little else to do other than apply a fresh dressing to the wound.

Sheriff Turner had been right about the road to Gartree being easy going and the town was reached three days after starting out and without incident. He had been told to ask for Sheriff Walter O'Leary who, according to Sheriff Turner, was a very untidy man who gave the appearance of allowing anyone to do anything they wanted to and who ran a very slack town. He was also told not to allow impressions to influence him too much and was assured that Walter O'Leary even knew whenever a new fly landed anywhere in town.

Sheriff Walter O'Leary certainly lived up to the picture painted by Sheriff Turner; a large, fat, bearded, dirty and very smelly man who gave the impression of having been poured into the chair behind the desk. He stared almost malevolently at the young deputy marshal and gave the occasional grunt as he listened to what Mick had to say but asked no questions.

'Sure, they was here,' O'Leary grunted. 'Stayed three days – or it could've been four, I ain't sure. Anyhow, it was obvious to me that they was outlaws but since that probably applies to almost everyone in this town, I didn't bother too much. They didn't cause no trouble an' they paid their bills so I left 'em alone. An' before you say anythin', I know maybe I should sometimes do more'n I do but I have enough problems runnin' this town without lookin' for even more trouble.'

'Which way did they go?' asked Mick, sighing as he realized that no matter what he said it would make little impression on O'Leary.

'Marshal,' grated the sheriff, 'There's only two ways in an' out of this god-forsaken hole. The first is the way you came in an' the second is due south alongside the river. I never saw 'em leave but my guess is they headed south since there don't seem much point in headin' back the way they came.'

'I came in from Coloma,' Mick pointed out, 'they rode in from Lindsay.'

'Same difference,' muttered O'Leary. 'The road from Lindsay joins the Coloma road about half a day out from here. Believe me, there just ain't no other way out of here unless you is kin to a mountain goat. You'll see what I mean when you leave.'

'Where does the road lead to?' Mick asked.

'McFarland is due south – just keep on followin' the river,' said O'Leary. 'There's a fork about a day out just after Red Lake Pass which goes off to Big Pine, although why the hell anybody would want to go to Big Pine I don't know. It's even worse'n here but it's mainly a ghost town left over after a gold rush about ten years ago. There's still a couple of miners there I think, but sod all else.'

'What's McFarland like?'

'Don't rightly know,' admitted O'Leary, 'Strange to say I ain't never been there, but I do hear say it's bigger'n Lindsay or Coloma. There's supposed to be an army fort there.'

Mick decided that he was not going to get any further information from Sheriff Walter O'Leary and certainly nothing of any use. Since it was now too late to consider moving on, he asked about a rooming-house and was directed to what he was assured was the best rooming-house in town. In fact it turned out to be the only rooming-house in town and it took little more than a cursory inspection to convince Mick that he would be better off sleeping in the forest. At least in the forest he knew who or what to expect as his bed-companions. However, he did visit what seemed to be the best of the three saloons in town, the only one which was built of part brick and part timber – the other two being little more than large tents.

As expected, the beer was warm and weak. What whiskey there was, although the genuine stuff, was very expensive and, as in so many of the more remote places, the main hard drink was rum. He chose the warm, weak beer which did not taste quite as bad as he had anticipated. His refusal of entertainment by a well-worn bar-girl was met with a mouthful of abuse until she noticed the badge pinned to his shirt.

'Deputy Marshal!' she said. 'Now what in the name of hell would bring a deputy marshal out here? I know most folk here is probably wanted for somethin' somewhere but I don't reckon any one of 'em has got a price of more'n fifty dollars, if that. I reckon most wouldn't fetch even twenty-five dollars. I'd say it wasn't worth anyone's bother comin' out here after the likes of them.'

'I'm not interested in anyone in town,' said Mick. 'I'm on the trail of two outlaws who really are worth somethin'. Maybe you saw 'em? Two men by the names of Saul Evans and Harold Buck.'

'So what's in it for me?' demanded the woman. 'You don't want me but you want what I might know. Everythin' has its price an' a girl has to make a livin' somehow.'

'Not a damned thing,' asserted Mick. 'I already know for sure they were here, I was just wonderin' if they talked to anyone, you know, like where they were goin'.'

'Sure, I remember them,' she sneered. 'They was just the same as you, real tight wads, even after they cleaned up on a dog fight. They tell me they won upwards of a thousand dollars bettin' on a dog what had no chance of winnin'.'

'Dog fight?' queried Mick.

'Sure, you know, two dogs fightin' each other,' she sneered again. 'Don't tell me you ain't never heard of dog fightin' or cock fightin'. Anyhow, they backed a dog what stood no chance but somehow it won – twice. Most folk reckon they must've got at the other dogs in some way. Old Lance over there...' she nodded in the direction of an old man sitting in a corner, 'he owned one of the dogs, best fightin' dog anyone's seen in these parts for many a year. He bet all his money on it winnin' an' lost the lot.'

'Maybe I'll talk to him,' said Mick. 'Thanks anyway.' The woman left him to try her luck with other customers and Mick wandered across to the old man.

It transpired that the old man had overheard Evans and Buck talking shortly before they left town and that the name Tenabo had been mentioned as their ultimate destination. Although Mick had never heard of such a place it appeared that the old man knew it well and that the only way to reach it from Gartree was through Big Pine but that Big Pine was a town best avoided, especially by law men even though hardly anyone lived there these days.

'I'd hide that badge of yours if you go through Big Pine, they'll shoot you as soon as look at you,' advised the old man. 'It might not be a bad idea to keep it hidden in Tenabo as well.'

At least Mick now knew that his quarry had a large amount of money but he was well aware that money and men like Evans and Buck were soon parted and that they would not be content until they had somehow disposed of it. Even so, spending that amount of money would take time, and Mick had a considerable amount of time to make up.

Big Pine's reputation appeared well founded and Mick's arrival was greeted in surly silence by the few inhabitants. He did wonder just how much they were all worth in reward money and had he had time he might have taken the idea further. He made a mental note for the future.

He did not bother attempting to make any enquiries, instead riding on through the town along the only road out. He did, however, heed the advice he had been given in Gartree and had removed his badge of office. A day and a half after leaving Big Pine he arrived in Tenabo, again with his marshal's badge in his pocket.

However, since there appeared to be at least three roads his quarry might have taken, he was forced to ask a few questions and since the town did not have a sheriff he went into the only bar where the bartender proved surprisingly helpful.

'You've just missed 'em,' he told Mick. 'They left town this mornin'. Headed out along the Dinuba road.'

'Dinuba?' queried Mick.

'Yeh. It ain't no place really, nothin' more'n a tradin' post,' confirmed the bartender. 'It used to be a way-station for the stagecoach but that stopped comin' this way more'n three years ago now. I don't think they really had any idea where they were goin'. If they had they wouldn't've gone that way, there's nothin' but mountains for more'n two hundred miles past there an' after that another two hundred miles of desert. Jake Harrington – he owns the place – makes his livin' tradin' furs with the Indians.'

'At least I know they're only half a day ahead,' said Mick.

'So what's your interest?' asked the bartender. 'My guess is they're outlaws on the run. Are you a bounty hunter or somethin'?'

'Somethin' like that,' nodded Mick. 'How far is to this Dinuba place?'

'Two days,' said the bartender.

Mick did not hang about, instead choosing to use what daylight was remaining to gain time and distance on the two.

The mountains actually started not long after he had left Tenabo. The trail meandered between towering hills and through narrow valleys and, sensing that he

145

was gaining ground rapidly, Mick pushed on well after sunset. He eventually pulled up for the night alongside a swift flowing river which he could hear rather than see but which he felt he would eventually have to cross. He did not fancy trying to negotiate it in the dark.

The morning light proved that he had been wise not to attempt a crossing the previous night. The trail plainly led down into the water about a mile further up from where he had camped and, although shallow, it was fast moving and was difficult enough to negotiate even in daylight.

Once on the opposite bank, the trees thinned out and half an hour later there were signs of the land having been cultivated. Ten minutes after the first signs of cultivation Mick found himself looking down on a log cabin set beside a small lake. Although smoke was coming from the chimney, something told him that all was not as serene as it appeared. There were no outward signs of trouble or problems, it was simply an almost overpowering feeling. Since there was no other choice but to ride down into the small valley, he held back, hiding amongst a clump of trees and studied the cabin.

For ten minutes nothing happened, but then the natural calm was shattered by a loud scream – a woman's scream. This was followed by coarse laughter and a single shot. Once again the woman's scream pierced the silence and a figure tumbled from the cabin laughing and firing his gun in the air. Mick felt a cold tingle along his spine and neck as he recognized the figure being that of Saul Evans. Without thinking, his rifle was at his shoulder and he was taking aim. Shooting and probably killing Saul Evans would have been very easy but another scream from inside the cabin made him check and lower the rifle.

Mick needed no telling as to what had happened; Evans and Buck had obviously come across the cabin the previous day and, true to their nature, had acted in the only way they knew how – brutally.

Saul Evans staggered towards a pump, held his head beneath it as he worked the handle, allowing the water to cascade over his head and shoulders. Again, shooting him would have been very easy but Mick was not prepared to risk the woman or anyone else inside the cabin being killed by Harold Buck, who had yet to show himself. A further cry from the cabin confirmed that the woman at least was still alive.

At first Mick settled down, prepared to wait until both outlaws were in the open and presenting easy targets but at the same time his concern for the occupants of the cabin dictated that he had to act quickly. He was quite certain that when the outlaws did eventually attempt to continue their journey they would kill everyone.

This conflict weighed heavily and although he thought about it, he knew that his priority was the safety of the occupants. His problem was how to get them assuming there were more than just the woman – away from the cabin or to get Buck and Evans away. He decided that the only way would be to let the outlaws know that he was there.

'Evans, Buck, this is as far as you go!' he called out. 'Give yourselves up.'

Saul Evans almost fell over as he twisted round, gun in hand. Mick heard a call from the cabin, though he was unable to hear what was said, but he saw the barrel of a rifle being pushed through a window.

'What's that you say?' demanded Evans.

'I said, give yourselves up,' repeated Mick. 'You tell Buck to let whoever you've got inside there go an' then tell him to come out with his hands up.' He was well aware that the chances of such a thing happening were zero, but he felt that he might prevent the murder of the woman.

'Hey, I know that voice!' shouted Evans, taking the opportunity to hide behind a pile of wood. 'It can't be though, you're dead, I shot you myself an' left your body by that river. Is that you, Nelson?'

'You'd better believe it,' responded Mick. 'Either that or you'd better start believin' in ghosts.'

'Harold!' Evans called. 'You hear that? That bastard Nelson ain't dead. I said we should've put another bullet through his head to make sure.'

'It can't be him,' responded Buck. 'His head was shattered, no man could've lived after that.'

'Then I guess that makes me a ghost,' called Mick. 'If I am a ghost I can't be killed again, so I guess you might as well give yourselves up.'

'OK,' shouted Buck, 'So you is still alive. It ain't goin' to do you much good though. We've got a woman an' two small kids here an' one man who's got a bullet in his chest an' should be dead by now. You back off, Nelson. If you don't they all die.'

'If they die you'll be close behind,' warned Mick.

'The choice is yours, Nelson,' called Evans who came out from behind the pile of logs. 'OK, you can shoot me if you've a mind to but everyone inside dies at the same time.' For a moment Mick was very tempted to shoot Evans and take a chance on what would happen next. He sighed and eased his finger off the trigger. 'We was just about to leave,' continued Evans. 'Now don't go doin' nothin' foolish. The woman comes with us at least until we're well away from here.'

'Leave her!' commanded Mick. 'I'll give you a good start.'

'No deal, Marshal,' responded Buck. 'She comes with us, just like we did with that girl. It's what they call insurance. Oh yeh, did you ever get the girl back?'

'She's probably back with her mother by now,' said Mick. 'I found her with the Germans, the ones you sold her to.'

'Easiest twenty dollars we ever made,' laughed Evans. 'OK, that's enough jawin', we're ridin' out of here, with the woman. You just make sure you hold back or she dies.'

'What guarantee do I have that you won't kill her anyhow?' said Mick.

'You don't have no guarantee at all,' laughed Evans. 'You'll just have to take our word for it.'

'That's like trustin' a rattlesnake not to bite,' sneered Mick. 'OK, I guess I don't have no choice.'

Saul Evans disappeared behind the cabin and the rifle protruding from the window also vanished. For a few moments there was silence. That silence was suddenly broken by the sound of horses racing away and Mick caught a brief glimpse of a woman clinging behind one of them.

Leaving his horse, he ran down the slope and burst through the cabin door. He was met by the sight of two small children, no more than five years old, sitting on a bed, clinging together and plainly terrified. On the floor in front of the open fire lay the body of a young, bearded man with a large bloodstain on his shirt. Mick ignored the children and went to the man.

He was still alive, although his breathing was very laboured, yet he was still conscious. He stared up at Mick for a moment and then smiled weakly before speaking in a whisper. Mick had replaced his marshal's badge and it was this which had made the man smile.

'Got here just in time,' the man croaked. 'They would've killed Liz an' the kids.' Mick did not tell him that his wife had been taken by the outlaws. 'I'll know better than try to pull a gun on the likes of them next time.'

'Let's get you on the bed,' said Mick. 'I want to take a look at that wound.'

'Liz is pretty good at things like that,' wheezed the man as Mick slid his arms under his body. 'She needs to be, livin' way out here.'

'Sure thing,' said Mick, lifting the man and transferring him to the bed. The children moved towards the head and cowered. 'Only problem with that is that your wife has been taken as hostage.'

The man's eyes flickered for a moment and then he nodded slightly. 'I guess I knew that,' he croaked. 'Leave me, you have to get her back if only for the kids' sake. I'll be OK.'

'Not until I've had a good look at you,' said Mick. 'What happens to your kids if you die?'

'Are you a doctor as well?' the man grinned, weakly. 'I'll be all right. There's an old Indian couple livin' up in a cave not far from here. The woman helped Liz when the children were born. You go fetch them, I'll be OK.'

There was logic in what the man said. Mick certainly knew nothing about medical matters and now that he was so close to Evans and Buck he did not want to lose even more time. After coaxing instructions on how to reach the cave from the man, he rode off. The cave was only a matter of half an hour away and in less than two hours the two old Indians had taken over the cabin and the children, who did not appear to be frightened of them at all.

Knowing that there was nothing else he could do, Mick rode off in pursuit of Saul Evans, Harold Buck and, more importantly, their hostage.

EIGHT

Following the outlaws' tracks proved very easy if only for the fact that there was only one way they could have gone. At regular intervals along the track there were some quite distinct signs which confirmed that Mick was on the right trail but, apart from one possibility about two hours after starting out, both theirs and Mick's route was dictated by the steep-sided mountains and narrow, tree-lined valleys. The one place where they might have taken a different route was very quickly ruled out when he discovered fresh hoof prints on the muddy bank of a small stream which crossed the track a little further on.

Ever conscious that they now had another hostage and convinced that they would not hesitate to kill her if they felt it necessary, caution played a large part in Mick's strategy. More than once he thought that he had heard them but on each occasion, after very cautious investigation, the sounds were found to have been made by either a bear or a deer. The deer presented no problems but he took care to give the bears a chance to get well away.

By nightfall it appeared that Evans and Buck were maintaining their distance and he somewhat reluctantly made camp alongside a fast-flowing stream. Although the night was very cold, he decided against lighting a fire just in case the glow should attract their attention and make him an easy target. He also took the opportunity to scale a high cliff which would give him a good view of the valley ahead, in the hope that they might have lit a fire. However, it seemed that they were either too far ahead or that they were also being cautious.

The following morning was also very cold, the sun not yet having penetrated the valley floor, but there was sufficient light for an early start. Two hours later he came across another fast-flowing stream where it seemed that they had also spent the night, there being very definite signs of several people having slept on the grass.

A short time later the valley widened out and a river appeared on his right although the very steep mountain sides still dictated which way the trail went. Half an hour later, he reached the end of that particular valley and found himself looking down on a small group of ramshackle buildings about half a mile away on a fairly wide, flat plain. He could only assume that this was Dinuba, the one-time way-station and now a trading post apparently owned by one Jake Harrington.

There were two horses tethered outside the larger of the buildings and Mick had the distinct feeling that he had at last caught up with the outlaws, although there were no other signs of life. Had it not been for the fact that they had the woman, he would have had little hesitation in riding in and forcing a showdown with the outlaws. As it was he hung back, partly hoping to confirm their presence, but also to study the area, looking for ways to approach without being seen, but it seemed that the closest he could get was no more than about 200 yards.

He had just come to the conclusion that perhaps he was being a little too cautious and that it was even possible that they were waiting for him, when he heard horses coming along the trail from the direction he had just come. He hid in a clump of bushes and waited.

Four Indians came into view, their horses laden with furs. Obviously they were going to the trading-post and Mick suddenly saw a way of reaching the post, hopefully without being seen. He mounted his horse and, just as the Indians had passed him, he rode out and joined them. They were plainly confused and even more so, it seemed, when they saw his marshal's badge. It soon became obvious that none of them could speak English and he simply nodded at them and indicated that they should continue. He manoeuvred his horse until he was in the middle of them and again indicated that they should continue. They chattered amongst themselves for a while but made no attempt to stop him.

His ruse appeared to be working; two figures emerged, one of whom Mick recognized as Harold Buck. He could not be certain as to the identity of the other since he was partly hidden by Buck, but he appeared outside the building and studied the approaching group. It seemed that he had not been seen, as both figures slowly turned and went back into the building. The group pulled up outside the building and the Indians looked at Mick, obviously wondering what he was going to do.

He leapt from his horse, leaving it untethered, and flattened himself against the wall, gun in hand. The Indians suddenly dismounted and ran for safety. Mick edged along the wall and peered through a grimy window.

Quite what he had expected, he did not know, but he had expected to see someone. As it was, the room, fairly large but cluttered with all manner of strange objects and with what appeared to be a bar or counter at one end, seemed completely empty. He waited a few moments but when it seemed that there was nobody in the room, he slowly opened the door, ever conscious that his next step could well be his last.

The inside was very dull and dingy apart from the faint glow of a large oil-lamp hanging from the roof. An enormous bear, teeth bared and arms akimbo, in the middle of the room, made him start and dive for cover behind a pile of sacks, but he quickly realized that the bear was stuffed and very dead. Apart from himself and the stuffed bear, the room seemed to be empty, but he had the distinct feeling that he was not alone.

'We thought you'd follow us,' a voice suddenly boomed through what had been otherwise an eerie silence. 'I'm surprised at you, Nelson, I didn't think you'd walk straight into a trap.'

'Neither did I,' said Mick, casting around for the source of the voice, Saul Evans.

'Good idea you had gettin' here though,' continued Evans, which allowed Mick to place him behind the bear. 'I didn't see you with them Indians. Harold did, but then my eyesight ain't much good these days.'

'Where's the woman?' demanded Mick.

'Safe,' said the voice of Harold Buck, apparently from behind a pile of evil-smelling furs just behind the bear. 'Which is more'n can be said for you. You must lead some kind of charmed life, Nelson. We'd've both taken bets that you were dead. This time though, we're goin' to make double certain.'

'Then you'd better get on with it,' said Mick. 'This is your second chance. You blew the first and I'll make darned sure you never get the chance again, so you'd better get on with it while you can.'

'I never met a man who asked to die before,' said Buck. 'OK, Mr Deputy Marshal, if that's the way you want it, prepare to die...'

A hail of bullets thudded into the sacks and the woodwork immediately behind Mick's head, forcing him to keep his head down. Mick did manage to get a couple of shots in but he was apparently firing at shadows. He was also conscious that Evans and Buck were trying to get into position to get a better shot at him. He fired several shots but once again it appeared that he was firing at shadows.

A small window suddenly shattered just above his head and he was about to shoot when a rifle appeared, pointing above his head. It fired a single bullet. Whoever had fired the shot was very good, at least it appeared so if the intended target had been the oil lamp hanging from the roof.

The oil lamp suddenly fell, crashing to the floor just behind the bear from where flames spread rapidly as the oil spilled. Most of it seemed to run in the direction of the bear and in a matter of seconds the stuffed animal was engulfed in flames.

In a very short space of time, the room was filled with thick, acrid, choking smoke as fur, dried hide and whatever material the bear was stuffed with quickly burned. The flames had also started to spread to other objects. It was not long before it was almost impossible to breathe and certainly impossible to see, mainly due to the dense smoke but partly due to the effect on Mick's eyes. He was just about to make a quick exit when he heard coughing, cursing and what seemed like furniture being moved.

Suddenly, he was aware of two dark figures racing through the door, firing wildly in his general direction and, before he could do much about it, he heard the sound of horses racing away. Whilst being grateful to whoever had fired at the lamp, he also cursed that once again he had lost the outlaws. His impulse was to run out and ride after them there and then but his chest was hurting after so much coughing and his eyes felt as though they had been burned out of their sockets.

Gasping for breath and blinded by the dense smoke, Mick staggered outside where he sank to his knees gulping in the fresh air. After a few minutes he staggered to his feet and returned to peer, watery-eyed, inside the building, now very concerned as to the safety of the woman.

The four Indians appeared and, covering their noses and mouths and armed with some blankets, immediately began the task of putting out the flames which had by that time spread to even more stock. Mick joined them and it took about ten minutes to douse the fire, after which he started looking for the woman.

He had not really given much thought as to what had happened to Jake Harrington but he found both him and the woman tied up in an adjacent small room. Apart from being obviously badly shaken by their experience and having suffered from the effects of the smoke, neither Jake nor the woman appeared otherwise any the worse for their ordeal.

He gave the woman time to recover her composure before questioning her. Although she claimed that she had been raped several times during the time she had been with the outlaws, she was far more concerned as to what had happened to her children and her husband. Mick assured her that the children were unharmed but that her husband was apparently badly injured and that he was being looked after by the Indians from the cave. This news obviously reassured her.

'I guess I'd better get you back to him,' said Mick. 'It's a pity though, I've been after them two for a long time and this is the closest I've been.'

The Indians were talking to Jake Harrington, who explained to Mick that one of them had shot out the oil lamp, which seemed to be stating the obvious. He also added that they only intervened out of their concern for Jake.

'Had it just been you they would have kept well out of it,' he said. 'This is the only place they can sell their furs though, so if anythin' had happened to me they'd've been unable to make a livin'.'

'I guessed there must be some other reason,' muttered Mick. 'There ain't that many white folk even who'd put themselves out for a lawman. Did I get here just in time or did they decide to make a stand 'cos they knew I was on their trail? I suppose they decided to make a stand, I can't see any other reason for them not ridin' on or tyin' you up. Maybe I should've expected somethin' like this.'

'That's what they said,' confirmed Jake. 'They said somethin' about thinkin' they'd killed you once before but that this time they were goin' to make sure.

'An' thanks to your friends here, they didn't,' said Mick. 'They said I seem to have a charmed life an' it looks like they were right.'

Jake shrugged his shoulders and went to inspect the damage to his store and goods and eventually pronounced that it could have been far worse. Mick helped Jake and the Indians to throw out the few items which were damaged beyond repair, including the stuffed bear which needed quite a bit of careful manhandling since it was still smouldering and was very hot.

'He's been with me ever since I've been here,' said Jake, sadly. 'I can't do much for him now though. He's survived bein' shot at, knifed an' even an arrow in his eye, but I guess fire was just a bit too much.'

Mick was not interested in the fate of the bear, his interest was purely in which direction the outlaws had taken. He had not actually seen the way they had gone, his eyes had been hurting from the effects of the smoke and he had been unable to see more than a few yards even when he did get outside. However, he had the impression that it was due south, although on looking about it appeared that there were several other routes they could have taken.

'So where are they likely to have gone from here?' he asked. 'I was told that from here on there was about two hundred miles of mountain an' then another two hundred miles of desert. I don't know if they knew that or not. I suspect not. They wouldn't be bothered about things like that.'

'Most likely they'll follow the river,' said Jake. 'I get the occasional stranger through here an' they all seem to think that's the best way, even when I tell 'em it ain't. Sure, it looks fine from here an' for the first fifteen miles it is, but after that you come to a wall of rock more'n two thousand feet sheer an' there just ain't no other way round apart from a canyon the river goes through an' I can assure you that no man has ever got through that canyon alive. There are other ways through the mountains, the main one bein' the old coach road.'

'Old coach road?' queried Mick, temporarily forgetting that this had once been a coaching stop.

'It ain't been used for a couple of years now an' I hear there's been couple of land-slides in places, but you should be able to get through. There's a couple more old way-stations up in the mountains but they ain't occupied these days, leastways not as far as I know. I did hear that gold was discovered up there somewhere an' that there was quite a town had grown up, but I don't know if it's still there or not. More often than not these places only last a few months. It's a certain fact that nobody came this way to get there an' nobody has come from there. I'd say the chances are your outlaws followed the river.'

'And by the time I get the woman back to her farm they will have realized their mistake and had time to double back,' sighed Mick. 'Do you know her?'

'Sure,' replied Jake. 'Everybody in these parts knows the Bowmans and everybody means the Indians an' me. They're the only white folk apart from me in this territory. I wouldn't worry yourself too much about Mrs Bowman, the Indians who just rode in will make sure she gets back to her farm all right.'

Mick had been hoping for just such news, but he double checked with Mrs Bowman. It seemed that she was quite happy to be escorted back by the Indians, telling Mick that all the Indians in the territory were friendly.

Half an hour later Mick was on his way. Jake Harrington had been talking to the four Indians and one of them rode alongside him, Jake having told Mick that this particular Indian was the best tracker there was and that he would soon discover exactly which direction the outlaws had taken.

Like Jake had seemed to think, Mick would have guessed that they had followed the river but it turned out that he would have been wrong. The tracker quickly found tracks, although Mick had to admit that he would not have been able to detect them, which led off away from the river and towards the mountains. Eventually the tracker indicated that that was as far as he could go and, smilingly, pointed at the towering cliffs not more than a mile away. From his actions it seemed that a lot of climbing would be involved.

Mick was not at all certain that he was following Evans and Buck and had some doubts as to whether or not the tracker really knew. He could see no reason why they had not followed the river even though he now knew that it eventually led to a dead-end and he even considered turning back. However, it seemed that the road he was now on was the old coach road and as he crossed a small stream, he saw distinct hoof prints in the wet ground. He mentally apologized to the tracker for having doubted his ability.

Evans and Buck had slightly more than one hour's start on him and he knew that they would be expecting him to follow. The effect was to slow him down as he warily surveyed the trail ahead. There were numerous points where they might have been able to ambush him and he laboriously checked out the more obvious places, all of which slowed him down and therefore increased the distance between them. The road eventually reached the mountains and, strangely enough, the places where he might have been ambushed became very infrequent.

This was due mainly to the fact that the road now followed the contours of the mountain and had a sheer cliff on one side and a sheer drop on the other as it climbed steadily upwards. It was very slow going and, as Jake had predicted, there were numerous places where the adjacent cliff had collapsed and Mick was forced to pick his way carefully over the rubble. There were signs that his quarry had also negotiated them.

By nightfall, still heading steadily upwards, he found a recess with water running down one part of it, and quite a lot of grass for his horse, where he decided to spend the night.

He resumed the chase shortly after dawn. The narrow road continued to climb steeply and, less than hour later, he came across another landslide, although this one appeared to be very recent and he wondered if Evans and Buck had caused it in some way.

Crossing the scree appeared very dangerous; the rock and rubble were very loose and his first tentative steps across it almost had him and his horse falling into an abyss of at least 3,000 feet. He quickly retraced his steps, from where he studied the obstacle. In the end he decided that he had either to clear himself a path or return down the track and find another way round. Since that would have meant returning to Dinuba and would have undoubtedly added several days to his journey, he opted for clearing a path.

The blockage was about thirty feet wide but even so it meant that he had many hours of hard work in front of him. He tethered his horse in a small recess and set to throwing rubble and boulders over the edge.

After more than four hours, he started to wonder if he had made the right choice. More than once he was beginning to think that he was making headway when more rock would slide into the space he had just cleared. However, after another four hours he suddenly realized that he was more than half-way across. By the time darkness was beginning to close in he had no more than another five or six feet to clear.

By that time his hands were swollen and bleeding and he very reluctantly decided that he must rest for the night and clear the remainder in the morning. Evans and Buck were now at least a day ahead of him.

Clearing the remaining rock and rubble continued at first light but it was another three hours before there was a clear, safe pathway. Although crossing seemed fairly easy, he nevertheless took great care since even putting one foot wrong could have led to him and his horse being plunged into the abyss. It was with a great sigh of relief that he found himself safely on the opposite side.

The trail continued upwards for another two hours, during which time he was forced to negotiate two other landslips, although neither presented any great problem. Eventually the trail levelled out on to flatter, treeless ground, passing through deep-sided gulleys as the flat ground gave way to mountain passes. He could see why the stagecoach company had abandoned this particular route.

There were numerous places where ambush would have been very easy but it seemed that the outlaws were simply intent on riding on. By nightfall he again camped alongside a small stream and this time he had no compunction in lighting a fire. Not to have done so might well have led to him freezing to death during the night. There was plenty of rough scrub to keep the fire going and sufficient grass for his horse but he was forced to go hungry, although he was very tempted to go after a group of mountain goats he had seen. Unfortunately the goats had also seen him and he knew that he would never get close enough.

He had been right to make a fire; when he awoke his limbs were very cold and very stiff and ice had formed at the edges of the stream. He added brush to the fire and took some time to warm himself before riding on. He was now so far behind the outlaws that another hour or two was not going to make that much difference.

It was very difficult to tell if he was still on the right trail or not since signs of progress left by Evans and Buck were non-existent as far as he was concerned. However, after another two hours following the twisting trail, he came across the cold ashes of a fire and had to assume that they had camped there. If they had stayed there, he realized that this would have been two days earlier, it was too close to have been the previous night. This meant that he was now two days behind.

After a time, he realized that the trail was now descending and at one point he caught a glimpse of what must have been the desert he had been told about. It appeared flat, treeless and stretched as far as the eye could see. Ten minutes after sighting the desert, he came across the remains of what must have been one of the now disused way-stations.

Hunger was now beginning to make him feel very weak and, out of nothing more than desperation, he searched the buildings, not really expecting to find anything. However, luck was on his side when he discovered a sack of dried beans, a well-dried and very leathery side of salt beef of unknown age and a large jar of pickled eggs.

The eggs at least seemed edible and he had heard that salt beef could keep for years if kept at the right temperature. He had no doubt that it was cool enough and dry enough up in the mountains for most of the year. After eating three of the eggs which made him feel very thirsty, he set about attempting to cook the beans and salt beef. Water presented no problem, there was a fast-flowing stream close to the buildings.

His efforts at creating something edible seemed to meet with some success, at least it did not taste too bad once he had cooked it and it certainly filled him up. The problems seemed to creep up on him about two hours later in the form of a stomach ache and diarrhoea. His opinion was that it had been the pickled eggs which were the cause of his discomfort.

From that point onwards, the trail turned in towards the mountains, although it was still mainly downhill and, unlike the ascent, it followed narrow valleys and gulleys for most of the way and he did not have any problems with landslips.

Shortly before sunset the road followed the side of a mountain on one of the rare occasions when he had a sheer drop on one side and a cliff on the other. It did not present any difficulties at all, but he suddenly noticed lights far below. He stopped to take a closer look.

It seemed that the lights came from what appeared to be a mass of tents. He could only assume that this was the new gold-rush town Jake Harrington had mentioned. Although the town looked so close, when he studied the road, he realized that he was, in fact, heading away. He had no doubt that

Evans and Buck would have made for the town and that was where he intended to go as well.

He followed the road for almost another hour until it became impossible to see, by which time he had left the lights of the town well behind. He opted to sleep the night up in the mountains and look for a way down at first light. He had brought the jar of pickled eggs, some beans and some salt beef with him but after his experience and discomfort earlier, he discarded the eggs and chewed on a leathery piece of beef. Once again he found enough brush-wood to make a fire and did not feel it necessary to hide his presence. He later discovered that perhaps it had not been the eggs which had caused his stomach upset.

NINE

It was almost an hour after starting off at dawn before Mick came across another trail. This one was plainly well used, leading off at a sharp angle from the main track and descending quite steeply at first. Thick mud made the track very treacherous and he was forced to travel very slowly, allowing the horse to find its own footing. He had to assume that it had rained recently since the surrounding trees were also dripping with water, although he had not encountered any. Eventually the descent eased, crossed a shallow, muddy river and joined another track which again seemed well used. Although this trail was largely on the level, it was still extremely muddy and very treacherous in parts. Two hours later, taking longer than he had expected, he found himself looking down upon a valley, part of which was covered by a mass of tents of varying sizes and two three-storey timber buildings all set amidst what could only be described as a sea of mud.

There was little room for doubt that this was the gold-rush town to which Jake Harrington had referred. The surrounding mountain sides were covered with flimsy looking sluices, makeshift screens and riddles and countless men digging out their claims in the hope of striking the elusive mother lode. Nobody seemed to give him a second glance as he made his way through the mud to the town.

Where the trail crossed the shallow river again and the tents started, someone had erected a rough sign which proclaimed the name of the town to be Gold Rock. Hardly an original name but Mick had to admit that it was probably appropriate.

At first all the tents seemed to be those where the miners lived but he eventually arrived at the first of the three-storey wooden buildings, which turned out to be a bar and gambling hall. Two tired looking women standing on the boardwalk suggested that he might like to relax after his journey, although they seemed almost relieved when he refused. One noticed his badge of office, nudged her companion, whispered something to her and then disappeared into the building.

The second wooden structure proved to

be a general store, apparently the only such store in the town. A smaller, lean-to building against the general store turned out to be the assay office, where gold was tested for purity and, if the miners needed to sell, would be bought on behalf of the state or government. It was at the general store that Mick decided to start his inquiries.

'Deputy Marshal Mick Nelson,' he said, introducing himself to the store owner. 'I'm looking for two outlaws, Saul Evans and Harold Buck.'

'You could be looking for the man in the moon as far as I'm concerned,' replied the store owner. 'Sam Laker, I own this place. Names don't mean much round here. A good many folk here don't use their right names, most of them have somethin' to hide I guess.'

'I don't think Evans and Buck have ever used other names,' said Mick. 'They might not even be here, it's just a hunch. I have to check it out though. If my information is right there ain't another town for at least another two hundred miles and I reckon they must know that by now so the chances are that they are either here or have been here in last day or two.'

'Three hundred,' corrected Sam Laker. 'Most of it is desert. Yeh, I guess you're probably right, there just ain't nowhere's else to go an' when the gold finally runs out here there'll be nowhere to go. So, you're a deputy marshal. You're the first lawman we've had through here. The law tends to ignore places like this. I guess they're more trouble than they're worth normally. Maybe it ain't a bad thing you're here though, it might make one or two of 'em sit up an' take notice. The only justice here is the gun or lynching when someone strays on to someone else's claim. It's usually a case of shoot first and ask questions later. You should've been here two days ago. A young feller was accused of stealin' off another claim. They strung him up on that tree by the river.' He indicated a large tree outside the store.

'Did he?' asked Mick.

'I don't rightly know,' said Sam. 'If he did I guess he asked for it. If he didn't, that was just his hard luck. Formalities like trials just don't happen. Mostly folk are caught in the act so it ain't a matter of provin' guilt. I don't think that happened with this young feller though, he just had the hard luck to be found nearby when the gold went missin'.'

'Very hard luck. He can't complain about

it now, can he?' nodded Mick. 'So you've not seen any strangers through here in the last two or three days? Fairly big men, clean shaven, or at least they were last time I saw them.'

'Lots of folk come into town clean shaven,' said Sam. 'Most give up on the idea when they've been here a few days. There is a feller set himself up as a barber and offers hot baths too, not that many folk bother with hot baths. Strangers? They come an' go every day. You're the fourth today as far as I know. Three fellers rode in this mornin' with a piece of paper which is supposed to give them rights to a claim. They're down at the assay office right now sortin' out exactly where it is.'

'I didn't think the assay people dealt with claims,' said Mick.

'It ain't unusual,' said Sam. 'They work for the government or the state so I guess they're the best people to sort things like that out.'

'How many people are there in this place?' asked Mick.

'Don't rightly know the answer to that either,' replied Sam. 'Personally I'd say you was lookin' at close on three thousand, maybe even more. About half are miners an' the rest either their women, hangers-on, gamblers, a few whores or businessmen like me.'

'That's a lot of people,' admitted Mick. 'I guess a man could search for days an' not find who he was lookin' for.'

'Most folk end up at the gamblin' hall at some time or another,' said Sam. 'I guess all you need to do is sit outside it an' let them come to you. There are a couple of other gamblin' places but they're just big tents. They play mainly cards but the one does have a roulette wheel. They don't have the other tables like Greg Thompson does though, nor the women, besides which he keeps a decent beer whereas the others just sell crude rum an' some rough moonshine whiskey.'

'I guess most folk end up here as well at some time or another,' said Mick. 'You look like the only store in town an' they will all need supplies from time to time.'

'That's not strictly true,' said Sam. 'There's a minin' supplies company out on the edge of town, you know, heavy stuff which I just couldn't deal with. There's a bakery just set up as well. I hear they're goin' to build a proper bakery but for the moment they work from a tent. Then there's a butcher. He hunts deer an' such like an' sells the meat. Most folk can't be bothered with doin' their own huntin', they're quite happy to pay big prices for butchered meat. A bootmaker set himself up a couple of weeks ago an' seems to be doin' good business. There's three eatin' houses as well. They do pretty good trade, leastways they seem to be full most of the time. Apart from that, I guess I sell everythin' else, anythin' from knives to pots an' pans, shirts, jeans an' dungarees, dried meat, beans, flour – apart from the flour the baker gets in. Salt, eggs when I can get 'em, coffee, sugar, fresh vegetables which come in about once a week. Explosives – except that a lot of that business has gone to the minin' company – guns and ammunition. Yeh, I guess you could say most folk need me sometime or another.'

'What about roomin'-houses?' asked Mick. 'If strangers are passin' through all the time they must need beds.'

'There's seven of 'em,' replied Sam. 'You can hardly call 'em roomin'-houses though. They're just big tents full of bunks an' sleepin' maybe forty men each. Are you lookin' for a bed?'

'I guess even deputy marshals need to

sleep somewhere at sometime or another,' said Mick. 'I was kinda hopin' for a proper room somewhere to myself though. What about the gamblin' hall, don't they put folk up?'

'Only by the hour,' said Sam, laughing. 'You have to rent a room an' a girl. Tell you what I'll do though, since you're a marshal. I don't normally do things like this, I wouldn't trust any man here not to rob me. I have a small room at the back of the store. It's empty at the moment but I can put a bed in for you. It ain't much but it's better'n nothin'. Anyhow, I wouldn't like your chances of survivin' a single night in one of them roomin'-houses once they know you're a lawman.'

'That's mighty decent of you,' said Mick. 'Won't it make things difficult for you though? I don't want to put you to any risk.'

'No bother,' assured Sam. 'You'll have to provide your own food though. There's plenty of good water in the butt outside for washin'. If you want a hot bath you'll have to go see the barber. The best eatin' house is the one just outside, it's the cheapest as well.'

'That'll be just fine,' said Mick. 'The only thing is I don't know how long I'll be here.

I hope it won't be too long though, I can think of places I'd rather be. How much are you goin' to charge for the room?'

'That's on me,' said Sam. 'I'll give you a key to the back door so's you can come an' go as you need to. You can keep your horse in the paddock at the back, I own that too. I normally charge two dollars a day for feed, but for you it'll be one dollar. You can keep your guns an' saddle an' any other gear in your room. I do have a shed where I store things like that for some folk for a charge of five dollars a week or part of a week.'

'You seem to have an eye for business,' said Mick, smiling. 'OK, Mr Laker, I'll take you up on the room. Don't you remember if you've taken any horses an' gear from a couple of strangers in the last day or two?'

'It's a more sure-fire way of makin' a few bucks than diggin' for it,' said Sam. 'There's been eight strangers left their horses an' gear in the past three days an' any of them could be the men you're lookin' for. I don't take too much notice of faces. I give each man a ticket for his horse an' another for his gear. All a man has to do is hand me a ticket an' I hand over the horse an' gear. I do know that it ain't always the same man who left the horse an' gear who picks it up. Some of 'em gamble things like that away. I also take things in pawn, you know, lend money against goods. Sometimes I never see the owners again but I never lend more'n half what an item's worth so I don't lose money. Still, that ain't none of my business. I'll show you the room.'

As expected, the room was fairly small, no more than eight feet by six feet, but it was quite adequate for Mick's immediate needs. He unsaddled his horse, left the saddle in the room and led the animal into the paddock. There were about a dozen other horses and, in the hope that he might recognize the horses ridden by Evans and Buck, he carefully examined each one.

None of the horses had any markings or any other indications that might identify them and he had not really expected anything else. Unless there were any definite markings or the horse was of an unusual colour, horses were all the same as far as he was concerned. Sam Laker also allowed him to look in the shed at the saddles and other gear. Again, there was little to indicate to whom each saddle belonged and a search of various saddle-bags failed to throw any light on who the owners might be.

Having settled in, Mick decided that he

might as well start his search for Evans and Buck and he began by visiting the eating house which was situated close to the general store. The smell of cooking reminded him that he was hungry and he was quite surprised to find that the owners of this eating house were Chinese. There was nothing unusual in Chinese people running an eating house, it was just that he had somehow not expected to find them out here. The food appeared good and he ordered a large venison steak. An excellent mug of coffee washed everything down, including the price of three dollars which he thought rather excessive.

His attempt to question the owners of the eating house, a thin Chinese man and two women, failed dismally as they did not really seem to understand him, although he had the distinct impression that it was more a case of not wanting to understand.

The tent next to the eating house was one of the gambling tents and even in early afternoon it was quite full. For the first time people seemed to notice his badge of office and for a few moments an uneasy silence fell upon everyone as they looked at him expectantly. He took the opportunity to scan all the faces and, not seeing Evans or Buck, turned and left. Immediately there was an excited babble of voices and at least four men slipped out, eyeing him warily.

Further along the street, after passing tents which were obviously used for living in, Mick came across the first of the so-called rooming-houses and was met by a large, bearded man with whom Mick would not have liked to have picked a fight.

'I heard we had a marshal in town,' growled the man. 'Are you lookin' for anyone in particular or has the law suddenly taken an interest in Gold Rock?'

'Two men,' replied Mick. 'Saul Evans and Harold Buck. I don't suppose the names mean much to you though.'

'Maybe they do, maybe they don't,' said the big man. 'What they wanted for?'

'Oh, just the usual stuff,' said Mick, smiling. 'Murder, rape, robbery, kidnapping. From what I've seen of the folk in this town so far, that could apply to most folk round here. I sure wouldn't want to pick a fist fight with any I've seen so far.'

'The miners might look a rough bunch,' said the big man, 'they work hard, play hard an' can be as mean as anyone when they have to be. On the whole though they're not as bad as they look. Most miners are good folk really provided they're left alone to go about their business. I can't say that about the drifters who come through though. They're only after a quick buck.'

'I ain't had that much to do with miners,' confessed Mick. 'I'm just goin' by what I see and hear. What about Evans an' Buck? Do the names mean anythin' to you?'

'The names Evans an' Buck don't mean a damned thing,' admitted the man. 'Only thing is, I was in the gamin' hall last night an' there was one feller who insisted that his name was Harold an' not Harry or just H. He was with a group of four others, all fairly new in town an' certainly not miners.'

'That sounds like it might be Harold Buck,' nodded Mick. 'He has this thing about his name bein' Harold. Any idea where they might be stayin'?'

'I know where two of the others were stayin',' replied the man. 'They're down at Limpy Grant's place. They could be stayin' there as well.'

'Do you know their names?'

'I think the one is called Ted Jones,' laughed the man. 'He might be called Ted but Jones sounds a bit dubious.'

'I know plenty of folk called Jones,' said Mick. 'Jones was my mother's name before she wed my pa. Still, maybe you're right. Where is this Limpy Grant's place?'

'Right next to the gamin' hall,' said the man. 'Oh, an' do me a favour, don't tell anybody I told you. It don't do to get involved in other folk's business, not if you want to stay alive.'

'I've never even seen you,' assured Mick.

'Oh yeh, one more thing,' added the man. 'I got the impression that this Harold feller had known at least two of the others before. They were talkin' like they was old friends.'

'I suppose even Evans an' Buck had some friends before,' nodded Mick.

This time as he walked along the muddy street, people were taking far greater interest in him. It was obvious that word had spread rapidly and he had no doubts that by that time Evans and Buck were fully aware of his presence.

Three large ladies barred his way and proceeded to tell him that it was about time that the law showed some interest in the town and that they hoped he was going to do something about clearing the gaming house of the evil of gambling and those 'fallen women'. Rather than argue with them or tell them that he was in town on other business, he assured them that he would see what he could do.

Some of the men also appeared to welcome his presence but a great many treated him very warily, some even deliberately avoiding meeting him by making sudden detours. It seemed that word of his approach had reached the gaming hall quite some time before he actually arrived. A well-dressed, middle-aged man stepped off the boardwalk to greet him.

'Welcome to Gold Rock, Marshal,' said Greg Thompson, the owner of the gambling hall. 'My girls told me you'd arrived. What brings you to this god-forsaken place?'

'Official business,' replied Mick. 'Don't worry, I'm not interested in you or your business, although I have been asked by some ladies to close you down.'

'The Misses Beverley,' smiled Thompson. 'They arrived just after the town was set up, preachin' the gospels and railing against the evils of drink and prostitutes. They're persistent, I'll say that for them. So what's this official business?'

'Outlaws,' said Mick.

'I reckon that could apply to a good many folk, especially the drifters an' some of the professional gamblers. I don't allow professional gamblers in my place. I run house tables and I don't allow any cheating, all my games are run fair and square. There's no need to run crooked tables, there are enough mug punters out there without having to cheat them. Besides, it's good for business when someone does win big.'

'Do the names Saul Evans and Harold Buck mean anythin' to you?' asked Mick. 'Maybe the name Ted Jones.'

Greg Thompson thought for a moment and slowly shook his head. 'Can't say that I've ever heard of 'em,' he said. 'That don't mean a thing though, I never ask folk their names. It could be that one of my girls might know though. You'd be surprised what some folk tell a woman in bed.'

'Can I talk to them?' suggested Mick.

'Sure, none of 'em are busy at the moment, come on inside,' said Thompson. 'I'm always ready to help the law when I can.'

There were a few men trying their luck at the tables and all of them eyed Mick warily as he was led to a small office at the rear of the building. It was noticeable that at least two of them left.

The girls, six of them, were not much help. Whether this was due to a natural reluctance on their part not to become involved or whether they genuinely did not know, Mick was uncertain. One seemed to remember a man who could have been Harold Buck, but she could not be sure and did not know where he was.

Mick's next idea was to locate the rooming-house belonging to Limpy Grant and Greg Thompson gave him directions. However, he had only just stepped off the boardwalk outside the gambling hall when five men suddenly appeared from behind a nearby tent.

'Don't give up, do you, Nelson?' grated Saul Evans. 'OK, we're here, take us if you can.' The few people who were about suddenly turned and fled when they saw the five men, each with his hand resting on the handle of his pistol, spread themselves into a semi-circle around Mick.

'No, I don't give up,' said Mick. 'That's my job.'

'You got lucky again back at that tradin' post,' added Harold Buck. 'It seems you've got more lives than a cat. I reckon you've just about used 'em all up this time. Do you think you can take all of us?'

Mick slowly looked round and realized that he was completely out-gunned and that the only way he was going to get out of this situation was to bluff his way out. He had serious doubts as to whether anyone else would come to his aid and he also doubted if anyone would take any action against the men if they did kill him.

'I see you need help,' he said. 'Too scared to face me on your own. I reckon I wouldn't have to look too far to find that they are wanted as well.'

'They're old buddies,' said Evans. 'We served time together. They don't like deputy marshals either.'

'It's your move, Nelson,' said Buck. 'We're fed up with you houndin' us, we might as well get this thing over with here an' now.'

'I reckon I could probably take two of you,' said Mick, more in bravado than actual certainty. 'I don't think I need tell you just who those two will be. I'd say it was your move, not mine.'

Mick was reasonably fast with a gun but even he did not really believe that he would be able to carry out his threat. The five men glanced at each other and Mick braced himself...

'Just the man we've been looking for!' The Misses Beverley suddenly marched determinedly in front of Mick and placed themselves between him and the other men. 'We hope you did something about this den of iniquity,' said one.

'We want to talk to you about other things as well,' said another. 'Come with us, we can't talk here.' She firmly grasped Mick's arm and he was steered past the outlaws. Mick raised no objection but he was rather more than surprised that the five men simply allowed it to happen.

He noticed that the Misses Beverley deliberately kept themselves between him and the men as they led him away. They took him to a large tent which was apparently where they lived. He was surprised to find the interior well furnished and more in keeping with a proper house.

'I thank you, ladies,' he said when they eventually released him. 'I hope you realize that you could have got yourselves killed out there.'

'The Good Lord is on our side,' said one of them, firmly. 'It was obvious that you were in no position to defend yourself, you were hopelessly outnumbered. The Good Lord, however, can never be outnumbered or outgunned. I take it that those were the men you were looking for. We knew that you must be looking for someone like that, they wouldn't send a deputy marshal to a place like Gold Rock just to keep the peace.'

'Two of them,' admitted Mick. 'I don't know who the other three are, but I'll bet they're outlaws as well.'

'Nothing more certain,' said another of the ladies. 'I think we were guided to you just in time. We were but instruments of the Lord.'

'I don't see why he should be bothered about the likes of me,' said Mick. 'I ain't exactly what you would call a regular God-fearin' man. In fact the last time I went to church was when my sister was married, more'n three years ago now.'

'I do so hate that phrase "God-fearing",' said one of them. 'You should be rejoicing in the name of God, not fearing Him. The fact that you might have neglected your religion does not necessarily make you a bad man. We were obviously sent to make certain that you were not killed.'

'I can only say that I'm most grateful to you and the Good Lord,' said Mick. 'He might be on my side but I doubt if you will always be around to carry out his bidding. I might get gunned down as soon as I walk out of here.'

'If He had intended that you should meet

your end by the bullet, He would not have intervened,' insisted one of them. 'He obviously intended you to live and to carry out your duty.'

'Yes indeed,' agreed one of her sisters. 'As unsavoury as it might be, He needs people like you to exact retribution upon the sinners of this world. Have no fear, Right is Might, He and you shall triumph.'

'I hope you're right,' mumbled Mick.

TEN

Mick left the Misses Beverley, not having quite as much faith as they seemed to have in either the will of God or his own ability. He had been around long enough to know that a well-aimed bullet was probably far more effective than any prayer. His ability was another matter. He was quite capable of handling a gun but his speed and agility were, as yet, largely untried and he was not particularly anxious to put them to the test. Accordingly, when he did eventually emerge on to the muddy street, his hand was on his gun ready to use it should it prove necessary.

It had started to rain again, this time very heavily, and negotiating the mud which now formed the main street was very hard, given the slight camber which made keeping foothold difficult. It appeared that the onset of the rain was enough to drive almost everyone under cover of either their own tents, the gambling halls or the eating houses. There were a few foolhardy people negotiating the mud in an attempt to reach other places but they were certainly not interested in him or his problems. However, he was more than surprised that there was no sign of Evans or Buck or their new companions and he eventually made his way back to the general store unhindered.

Word of what had happened had reached the ears of Sam Laker, the general store owner, and he expressed some surprise that Mick had made it back safely. Mick, however, was taking no chances and once in his room he placed both his rifle and his pistol where they could be easily reached if needed. Sam was of the opinion that the outlaws would not make another attempt on his life again that night, declaring that no man in his right mind would be out in such weather. Mick pointed out that, in his opinion, neither Evans nor Buck were in their right minds.

Shortly after he'd got into bed, a clap of thunder shook the general store and the rain came down even more heavily. Even if he had accepted that there would be no further attempt on his life that night, the thunder and driving rain continued for what seemed most of the night, making a full night's sleep almost impossible. He realized that he must have dropped off to sleep on several occasions, only to be rudely awakened by a sudden, extra loud clap of thunder which had him snatching at his gun in the befuddled belief that someone was shooting at him. It proved to be a long night.

At first it was difficult to tell if it was dawn or not; it was still raining hard although the thunderstorm seemed to have passed. A blanket of heavy cloud shrouded the mountain-sides, cutting down the light. Peering out of the small window in his room, he decided that it must be dawn since he could make out nearby tents and a few dishevelled people. The sound of Sam Laker moving about appeared to confirm the arrival of the morning.

'There won't be many out workin' their claims this mornin',' said Sam as Mick opened the door into the store. 'I hear tell that a lot of tents down by Greg Thompson's place and the river got washed away during the night. That was sure some storm, the worst we've had since I've been here and I've seen a few. I reckon there's more to come as well.'

'I hope you're wrong about that,' observed Mick. 'Somebody must have been up early for you to hear about the damage. It's still pouring down.'

'A couple of miners were hammerin' on my door before dawn,' explained Sam. 'They'd lost their tent when the river started to flood. They wanted to know if I had another. They were lucky, I'd got three left. There'll be even more folk round wantin' to replace things they've lost or had damaged beyond repair.'

'I suppose other folk's losses are your gain,' observed Mick. 'What about the horses in the paddock, are they all right?'

'They seem to be,' said Sam. 'I ain't actually been out to check, but they look OK from the window.'

'I'll go check,' said Mick.

Apart from being very wet and looking thoroughly miserable, the horses did not appear to be any the worse for their experience. The hay which had been put out for them had been trampled into the mud during the night. Without asking Sam, Mick took more hay from under a tarpaulin and threw it over the fence. Seeing the horses eating reminded him that he too was feeling hungry.

From the door of the general store he could see that the eating house owned by the Chinese had also suffered damage and that it was obvious that it would not be open for business for quite some time. Sam Laker came to the rescue by offering Mick some ham and eggs, an offer which was gratefully accepted.

The rain stopped about an hour later and Mick took the opportunity to venture out, armed with his pistol and rifle. The rifle and pistol were merely a precaution, he was, in fact, rather more concerned as to the fate of the Misses Beverley than looking for Evans and Buck.

It seemed that hardly any tents had escaped damage in one form or another. In the vast majority of cases this appeared to amount to little more than having mud and water run through them and most of the occupants were now in the process of drying out. A few tents had been ripped by the high wind and one or two which had been close to the river had disappeared completely. The water level had risen at least five feet and appeared to be still rising. The other eating houses were also closed as they dried out, although there were queues of people waiting hopefully.

Mick eventually reached the tent belonging to the Misses Beverley and discovered that they seemed to have escaped any real damage, something the sisters put down to the will of God. Mick was not quite so certain, but it did appear that whilst all around had suffered greatly, the sisters had not. They thanked him for his concern but refused his offer of help, reminding him that he had more important work to do.

There had been no sign of Evans or Buck, although in the general mêlée of mud-covered people it was largely impossible to identify anyone in particular. However, he did check with Limpy Grant who assured him that they were still around but that he had no idea where they were at that moment. Limpy Grant's rooming-house was also one of the few tents at that end of town which had not been damaged to any great extent since it consisted of a stout wooden frame with only the roof and upper sides being of canvas.

Looking about, Mick rapidly came to the conclusion that he had seen enough mud to last him a lifetime. He was quite determined to get his business over and done with as soon as possible. With that objective in mind, he set about searching for the two outlaws.

His search was slow, made more difficult by

the mud. After what seemed like an hour, he came to the conclusion that neither of the outlaws was in the main part of the town. His search eventually took him along the river, upstream of the town and among the mine workings. There were one or two miners about, not working their claims, but assessing or repairing damage or attempting to bail out water. He could not help but think that such a thing was a complete waste of time and effort since water was continuously pouring off the hillside. He was about to return to the town when one of the miners called to him.

'You're that marshal ain't you?' said the man. 'I hear you is lookin' for some outlaws.'

'Do you know them?' asked Mick.

'I knows one of 'em,' grunted the miner. 'The one they call Saul cheated me out of almost a thousand dollars' worth of gold at cards. Couldn't prove nothin' though but I know he was cheatin' me. Men die for cheatin' at cards in these parts.'

'Maybe it's as well you didn't catch him cheatin',' said Mick. 'The chances are that it would've been you who'd been killed. Murder is their business. Have you seen him?'

'I seen him,' confirmed the miner. 'I seen him less'n ten minutes ago.'

'Where?' asked Mick.

'Him an' his friends is up there,' said the man, nodding behind him up the hill. 'One of 'em said that you'd be lookin' for 'em an' he said to tell you where they was.'

'OK, so you told me,' said Mick. 'There's a lot of places up there. Where are they exactly?'

'Don't know, didn't ask an' didn't see,' replied the miner. 'It ain't my business.'

Mick looked up at the hillside but, apart from two other miners, he could not see anyone. It seemed that Evans and Buck had chosen their site for a showdown very well if that was their intention. There did not appear to be any way he could approach without being seen. He could, of course, simply remain where he was and wait for them to come to him. A glance at the sky showed that clouds were gathering again and another rainstorm appeared imminent, as Sam Laker had predicted.

A few spots of rain made the decision as to what to do next a formality. There was no way he was going to risk climbing the hill in the rain and even without the rain he would have thought twice. As much as he wanted to bring his business to a conclusion, he realized that conditions were against him. He decided to return to the town and either wait for the storm to pass and then look for them or, as seemed the more obvious thing to do, wait for the outlaws to come to him.

'I'll be in the gamin' hall!' he called out, uncertain even that his voice had carried against the rising wind. A single shot echoed around although he did not see any sign of where the bullet landed. He assumed that the outlaws had heard him and that the shot was their response. He studied the hillside for a few moments but was unable to see them. 'You'll have to do better'n that,' he called again before making his way to the gaming hall.

There were not as many people in the gaming hall as he had expected and the bartender seemed to think that most were salvaging or drying out their possessions. Mick ordered a beer and sat in a corner alongside a window from where, hopefully, he would be able to see anyone who approached. It was about two hours and three beers later before he saw Harold Buck and two of the other men standing on the opposite side of the street, sheltering under one of the few trees.

In the meantime the storm had broken, although it did not seem as intense as it had been during the night. Flashes of lightning briefly lit up the area followed by claps of thunder which shook the building. The street between the gaming hall and the men opposite was nothing more than a river of thick mud and one man crossing it showed that it was at least a foot deep. It took him almost five minutes to negotiate the ten yards or so. Mick was quite satisfied that Buck and his companions would not attempt to cross. However, there were still two others whose whereabouts were unknown: Saul Evans and the third man.

The man who had just negotiated the street burst into the room, swearing and stamping his feet, demanding a beer. Mick turned to look briefly and when he again looked through the window Harold Buck and one of the other men had disappeared leaving only one man to watch him. Mick silently cursed the man who had entered the room for distracting him.

Thinking about it later, Mick realized that in sitting by the window he had presented himself as an easy target. Outside it was dark, inside it was light, making it easier for anyone looking in to see inside. This apparent oversight was suddenly brought home to him.

The window shattered into a myriad pieces and at least three bullets ripped into the table at which Mick was sitting. What happened next was largely a matter of pure instinct on Mick's part as he found himself crouching behind another table which had somehow become upended. His pistol was in his hand, although he did not remember drawing it. Another hail of bullets shattered the woodwork of the table and one lodged in the wall close to his ear.

He was just about to take aim at a shadowy figure which he thought he could see at the window when there was another hail of bullets, this time from the doorway. He was just in time to see two figures dart behind one of the gaming tables. He had to assume that Saul Evans and the third man had entered the room.

The few people who had been in the room seemed to have disappeared. In fact they were all crouching behind gaming tables. A couple of girls who had been hanging about the bar had also disappeared.

'You is dead meat, Nelson!' called Saul Evans. 'There ain't no interferin' women to get you out of this now.'

'I seem to remember you thinkin' I was dead meat more'n once before,' called Mick. 'Maybe I am dead, maybe you're tryin' to kill a ghost.'

'This time I'll make double sure,' snarled Evans. 'I'll blow your brains right out just to be certain.'

'At least I've got some brains to blow out, which is more'n you have, Evans,' called Mick. 'First though, you have to get close enough.' The response came in the form of several shots at the table. This was followed by several more shots from the direction of the broken window. A quick glance round the room showed the other occupants crouching behind tables, a couple with guns in hand. However, Mick knew enough about human nature to realize that he was effectively on his own.

At first sight there appeared to be nothing he could do; any movement away from his cover would place him in direct line of fire. His only chance seemed to lie in somehow creating a diversion. Exactly how that diversion could be achieved seemed, at first glance, to be impossible. Eventually, however, the germ of an idea started to form in his mind.

The room was lit by several large oil lamps hanging from the roof. If he could shoot out the lamps, the ensuing relative darkness might serve to provide him with the opportunity to move. Taking careful aim at the lamp nearest the door, he fired. The result was rather different from that which he had expected. His shot was accurate enough, the oil lamp shattered but it also sent the oil pouring on to the floor and somehow it caught fire. This sent Saul Evans and his companion dashing for fresh cover as the flames quickly took a hold.

Mick grunted with satisfaction and aimed at one of the lamps hanging over the bar. This time he tried to make certain that it also caught fire. Although things did not happen as he had intended, he did succeed in making the oil spill on to the bar. He fired at a second lamp above the counter, this time at the bracket supporting it. His shot was very accurate and the lamp shattered on to the bar, ignited and immediately lit the previously spilt oil, setting the whole counter ablaze. His next shot was at a lamp hanging near the shattered window and again he rather surprised himself with his accuracy. Once again flames spread along the floor, gradually engulfing the woodwork around the window.

The flames were now spreading rapidly along the dry flooring towards him. The previously cowering occupants of the bar suddenly leapt from their hiding places and raced for the door. In the general confusion Mick took the opportunity to change his place to another upturned table nearer the centre of the room. There were still several lamps and Mick concentrated on shooting them down. Three spilled their contents but did not ignite, the remaining two shattered on to the floor and flames rapidly spread, eventually engulfing the previously spilled oil.

By that time thick, choking smoke filled the room and the screams of several women could be plainly heard as panic set in. Exactly where the outlaws were, Mick had no idea and at that moment their location was unimportant. He was, in fact, rapidly becoming surrounded by flames and was in danger of completing the task the outlaws had set out to do by burning himself to death.

Holding his hand over his nose and mouth, he made a dash for a door alongside the bar, hoping that it led to the outside. He thought he heard some shooting as he ran, but he made it to the door unscathed.

The door opened up in to a room with no other way out except a small window which did not seem large enough for him to squeeze through. However, he very quickly made the gap large enough by dragging a nearby table to the window, standing on it and then kicking out the frame.

The drop on the other side was higher than he had expected and a sharp pain in his ankle made him cry out as he landed. There was no time to see what damage he had done and after some agonizing minutes, he found himself lying under one of the few remaining trees in the town. He looked back to see that the entire building was engulfed in flame.

By that time, even though it was still raining heavily, it seemed that almost the entire population of the town had ventured out, most simply standing around staring. A few had heeded Greg Thompson's cries for help and were making futile efforts to quench the fire. Mick took the opportunity to examine his ankle and, while he was reasonably sure that he had not broken it, it was plainly badly sprained.

Although there were a lot of onlookers around him, it appeared that hardly anyone noticed his presence and the few who did hardly gave him a second glance. He struggled to his feet and gingerly tested his weight on the injured ankle. It hurt, but it was just about bearable. He watched the flames devour the building for a few minutes before turning his thoughts back to Evans and Buck.

As he made his way slowly through the crowds, it was plain that trying to locate anyone in particular was going to be something of a difficult task. More than once he thought he had seen one of them only to discover that it was someone else. By that time the rain was easing off, which simply served to encourage even more on-lookers. After about twenty minutes he came across the Misses Beverley.

'I think we are right in assuming that you had a hand in this,' said one of them, nodding in the direction of the burning gaming hall. There was a very satisfied look on all their faces.

'I guess you could say that,' admitted Mick. 'I reckon you'll be just about the only folk in town who won't mind though.'

'Mr Thompson had it coming to him,' said one of the other sisters with a wry smile. 'Unfortunately though, it will probably soon be rebuilt. We understand that those men had you ... how do you say it ... pinned down?'

'Just like they thought they had more'n once before,' said Mick. 'I'm lookin' for them.'

'And once again the Good Lord showed you a way out,' smiled the third sister. 'At the same time He destroyed that den of evil, although I do not think that Mr Thompson will understand the message. Men like that never do. I do believe that I saw Mr Evans and Mr Buck standing outside Mr Grant's so-called rooming-house only a few minutes ago.'

'Thanks,' said Mick. 'Now, if you'll excuse me, ladies, I have a job to finish.'

'We shall not wish you luck, Mr Nelson. With the Good Lord helping you, you will not have to rely on luck,' said the elder sister. 'With His help you will destroy these men.'

'Ladies,' grinned Mick. 'If I didn't know better I'd say you were actually enjoying all this mayhem and even relishing the prospect of my killing those men.'

'The Lord moves in mysterious ways, Mr Nelson,' she replied with a knowing grin. 'You and we are but small pieces in His great plan.'

'I wish he'd let me in on just a small part of it occasionally,' said Mick. 'Now, I must find those outlaws.'

The rain had now stopped completely, although water and mud still flowed freely making any form of upright stance rather difficult. In his case the problem was not helped by the condition of his ankle and several times he was forced to stop and allow the pain to ease.

He reached Limpy Grant's place only to discover that all five men had apparently split up and were searching for him. After struggling through the mud for about another five minutes, the pain in his ankle became unbearable. Since he was now at the top of a small hill behind the still-burning gaming hall, he opted to stay where he was and once again wait for the outlaws to come to him. He sat on a large rock making no attempt to hide himself.

Mick became aware that the crowd was beginning to disperse as interest in the burning building waned. Eventually almost everyone had returned to the task of sorting out their own problems. As the last few stragglers slithered down the slope away from him, Mick suddenly became aware that five figures remained, all looking up at him.

'I'm still here,' Mick goaded as the five slowly spread out to face him from about thirty yards away. 'I think my brains are still intact as well.'

'Not for much longer, Nelson,' called Harold Buck. 'You can't take out five of us. Prepare to die.'

'Maybe you're right about that,' called Mick. 'The question is which of you will die before I do.' If this comment did not have much effect on either Evans or Buck, it was apparent that it did make the other three falter slightly. This did not go unnoticed by Mick. 'This is between them two an' me,' he called again. 'More'n likely you three are wanted as well, but that's somethin' I don't know about. The best thing you can do is get the hell out of here while you can, I sure won't go lookin' for you.' Once again the three appeared to falter. 'There ain't no sense in gettin' yourselves killed over somethin' that don't concern you.'

'They're with us,' shouted Evans.

The five men started to advance up the muddy slope, obviously finding it difficult to maintain a foothold. It was very noticeable that Evans and Buck were allowed to

217

take the lead. They were now just about within pistol range, although Mick waited for one of them to make the first move.

The first shot appeared to have been made by Harold Buck but the bullet went wide. Mick's first answering shot also went wide but suddenly he was aware of several bullets embedding themselves into the mud close by. Mick leapt to his feet, knowing that he could shoot better from an upright stance. His second shot obviously struck home, apparently much to the surprise of Evans who cried out and dropped to the ground. It was obvious that he was not dead as he rolled over. A hail of shots followed but somehow all missed their target. Mick was past caring about himself and was determined that he was going to kill both Evans and Buck.

He took aim at Harold Buck but suddenly his ankle gave way and he found himself sliding rapidly down the muddy slope towards the men. This seemed to catch them off guard and two of them simply stood wide eyed as Mick careered into them, knocking both of them over. He recovered his composure just in time to see Harold Buck taking aim at him.

He did not remember raising his gun, but suddenly Buck cried out and fell to the ground. Mick vaguely remembered the other three men suddenly slithering down the hill away from him. As he struggled to his feet he saw Evans, now covered in mud, raise his pistol. Once again his ankle gave way...

The light was blinding but the voices somewhere overhead were familiar. As his eyes focused he realized that he was on a bed in the tent belonging to the Misses Beverley.

'What happened?' he croaked, conscious of a pain in his head.

'You almost got yourself killed, that's what happened,' replied the eldest sister. 'You were lucky we were around. A bullet hit your head. Just a scratch.' It certainly did not feel like a scratch to Mick.

'The outlaws?' he croaked again.

'Three of them ran off,' replied another sister. 'The last we saw of them they were riding out of town. I don't think we shall be bothered with them again.'

'Evans and Buck?'

'Both dead,' said the third sister. 'Mr Evans died about half an hour ago. You apparently shot him in the chest. Unfortunately we were forced to deal with Mr Buck.'

'You killed him?' gasped Mick in disbelief.

'As I say,' continued the third sister, 'we were forced to. Had we not you would most certainly have also died. The other three ran off when we appeared.'

'I thought the Lord was on my side,' said Mick. 'According to you he would have looked after me. That's what you are always saying.'

'And we also said that He needs help from time to time,' said the eldest sister. 'We are but tools in His hands. Through us He looked after you.'

'But you killed a man,' said Mick. 'I thought you were against things like that?'

'And so we are,' insisted the third sister. 'We do not intend making a habit of shooting people.'

Mick somehow managed to smile. He had to admire the way the Misses Beverley were able to justify everything in the name of the Lord.

'Which one of you actually fired the shot?' he asked.

'All of us,' they replied in unison.

Two days later Mick left Gold Rock. News

of what the Misses Beverley had done had spread rapidly, resulting in vastly increased attendances at their prayer meetings. It also resulted in a steady stream of proposals of marriage, all of which were firmly refused.

As Mick paused to look back on the town, the one thought in his mind was that he would never again want to see a storm like the one he had experienced and that he would never want to set foot in another town like Gold Rock. As for the Misses Beverley, he doubted very much if he would ever come across their like again.